Tales from the Sunday House

Tales from the
Sunday House

Minetta Altgelt Goyne

Foreword by James Ward Lee

Texas Christian University Press
Fort Worth

Library of Congress Cataloging-in-Publication Data

Goyne, Minetta Altgelt, 1924-1992
Tales from the Sunday house / by Minetta Altgelt Goyne :
Foreword by James Ward Lee
p.   cm.
ISBN 0-87565-173-9
1. German Americans—Texas—Social life and customs—Fiction.
I. Title
PS3557.097T35   1997   96-31689
CIP

Contents

Foreword
by James Ward Lee

*I*n the middle of the nineteenth century more than 7,000 Germans migrated to Central Texas—most to Comal, Gillespie, and Llano counties. The largest wave of German immigrants came under the sponsorship of a society called the Adelsverein led by Prince Carl of Solms-Braunfels. The first town established was New Braunfels in what is now Comal County. Shortly thereafter, John O. Meusebach led 120 settlers westward and founded Fredericksburg, now the county seat of Gillespie County. Those two cities have remained at the heart of "German Texas," though German immigrants continued to come throughout the nineteenth century and settle in all parts of the state.

For the next three-quarters of a century, the Germans of Central Texas retained much of their ethnicity: they were taught German in the schools, there were German-language newspapers, and ties to the Fatherland remained strong. But with the coming of World War I, many of the Hill Country Germans began slipping away from the old ways. The generation that grew up between the two world wars became more and more Americanized. It is the between-the-wars generation that Minetta Altgelt Goyne knew best and which informs the stories in *Tales from the Sunday House.*

In the eleven stories that make up the book, Mrs. Goyne gives us glimpses into the real lives of her parents' generation and her own. Her stories immerse us in the personal, private, and sometimes public lives of the Kreutz and Bracht families. Mrs. Goyne's stories are the kind of tales family members told other—often younger—members of the family as they sat by the fireside or on the porches of their "Sunday Houses," structures peculiar to the German Texans. Sunday Houses were built on the town lots that early settlers were given as part of their land grants. It was assumed by the leaders of the immigrant companies that the settlers would follow the European tradition of living in town and working the outlying farms. But given the distances the settlers would have to travel to work the fields, most built their homes on the farms and ranches they were developing. However, as time passed, many German farmers built Sunday Houses on their town lots so that they would have a place to rest when conducting business in town, attending to medical needs, or attending church services. Oftentimes, as the older residents retired from their farms and ranches, they moved permanently to their

Sunday Houses and left their rural homes to the younger generation. The architecture of the early Sunday Houses was simple, usually a one-room building with a porch attached and a sleeping loft in the attic. As the families grew and prospered, additions were made to the Sunday Houses so that some became much more elaborate buildings than the early cabins. Fredericksburg still has a number of Sunday Houses, and at least one remains in the Comal Town section of New Braunfels—the town where Minetta Altgelt Goyne grew up—which furnishes the setting for her stories about the Kreutz and Bracht families.

The tales told in this volume are exactly the kind of family stories that would have been told as families gathered in the Sunday House after church services. Sometimes incomplete, sometimes apparently pointless, sometimes merely addenda to previously told tales, Mrs. Goyne's *Tales from the Sunday House* do not always follow the beginning-middle-end formula of traditional fiction. For instance, at the end of "Masterpiece," we don't know whether Amalie Bracht (neé Kreutz) will survive her operation for the brain tumor that is blinding her. But since she turns up—apparently in the best of health—in later stories, we must assume that the surgery was successful. Nor do we know whether Otto Karl Kreutz, who first appears as a newborn in "The Scion," will go through life being branded "a sissy" as he is in "What Will People Think?" Even when we see him in uniform during World War II, there is still a question about his androgynous nature. We are never to know more. Since these stories are told by a cautious and reserved narrator to a similarly reserved audience (the family), it would be out of character for the narrator to be explicit about Karl's possible effeminacy.

Because the stories are told to an audience generally familiar with family and local history, we as readers have to be satisfied to be eavesdroppers. It is a technique seen in William Faulkner and other southern storytellers, a technique that allows us to overhear a narrator talking to a listener who is familiar with the context if not the particular story. In Faulkner's case, the culture of the novels and stories is the hill country of northern Mississippi, a land peopled by Scotch-Irish, English, and African Americans; in Minetta Altgelt Goyne's the culture is Teutonic and the people mostly pure Germans. Still, all are Americans by the time Faulkner and Ms. Goyne take up their stories. One of the characters in *Tales from the Sunday House* "thought himself as securely pedigreed as if his ancestors had come over on the Mayflower in 1620 instead of on the *Johann Dethart* in 1844."

By the time of the "Sunday House" stories, which take place roughly between 1920 and 1945, the German Texans had been in the country for three or four generations. Many of the old traditions remain, but as we learn in "Someday, *Vielleicht*,"

> Ever since the children had left home, they had showed a certain reluctance to speak German, and this had become something of a barrier between them and their parents, who did not realize that they themselves could not speak either language without the aid of the other one.

The German language was taught in many of the most heavily Germanic schools of the Hill Country until World War II, and the *Neu Braunfelser Zeitung* was printed in German until 1957.

The fact that Mrs. Goyne's original text did not translate the many German passages that the editors have glossed in this edition underlines at least two of the important motifs of the stories: that in the changing times of the mid-twentieth century more and more people regularly shifted back and forth between German and English (a generation or two before, many of the older residents would have known only German); and that these stories have as one of their motifs the story for a limited audience—the family or the natives of a still-German culture. But since the stories have both a regional and a universal appeal, the editors thought a translation would neither spoil Ms. Goyne's effect nor impede a reader caught up in the lives of the Kreutz and Bracht families.

The reader of Ms. Goyne's "Sunday House" stories will see a number of threads interwoven into some otherwise simple and quiet tales. We see the culture of the Hill Country Germans gradually change from German to American. In the first story, "Kaffeeklatsch," Hedwig Kreutz is very much the stereotypical German Hausfrau as she waits anxiously for her friends to arrive for their regular coffee and gossip session. Her house is immaculate, but she worries that some of her friends will detect a speck of dust. Her food "was so perfectly prepared that" her husband, Otto, can not imagine that she has any cause for worry. But when one of the guests brushes a speck of imaginary dust off a dropped skein of thread and exclaims, "Isn't it difficult to keep a house clean in this dry climate!" Hedwig is crushed. "Knowing she had mopped and dusted the entire house thoroughly just that morning, Hedwig struggled to keep her face serene. . . . How could Charlotte Gross presume to say such things, when Hedwig had once seen her replace an unsoiled but used saucer in the cupboard without washing it first!"

Thus begins the series of family stories that center on the Kreutz family—Hedwig and Otto, the older generation; their children Martin, Amalie, and Anna; Otto Karl, the son of Martin and Frieda, who is born in "The Scion." In "The Masterpiece," we meet Amalie, her husband, Fred Bracht, and their children: Johanne, Franz, Elspeth, and Annalies. Most of the stories in the volume follow these families and their developing lives in New Braunfels and vicinity. One story, though, focuses on a Chamber of Commerce go-getter, Jesse Kincaid, who has big plans for the city. Jesse, in "The Man with Big Ideas," has persuaded the Philadelphia Phillies to hold spring training in New Braunfels. Another story is about an explosion that occurs when Jesús Cantú accidentally takes a blasting cap home from Fred Bracht's quarry only to have his children let it get in a fire and cause an explosion which kills one of Cantú's children. Perhaps the most affecting chapter is "Twilight," made up largely of letters between Gustav Bracht and Ferdinand Renner. The two oldsters are now housebound and must communicate across New Braunfels by letter. The time is 1945, Germany is going down to defeat, and the two old men write about their decrepitude, how badly Germany has been bombed, and which of the New Braunfels boys are now fighting against the Fatherland.

In the final chapter, "Auf Wiedersehen," we get a summary of what has happened in the last twenty years—Otto and Hedwig are now dead, many members of the Kreutz-Bracht clan are serving in U. S. forces, and Karl Otto Kreutz—"The Scion"—is an army officer about to be sent to Germany to serve in the Occupation. On his final night at home, he attends a reunion dance at the high school where many of his fears and worries cause him to re-think his place in the life of New Braunfels. By the final chapter, the quiet and simple stories—tales suitable for any German Texan Sunday House—have given us an insight into the culture established by the early German immigrants and altered by the growing American-ness of the younger generations.

Preface

In studying the principles of creative writing, I became increasingly aware that working with that with which one is most familiar usually proves most successful. Consequently, my choice of a thesis was almost pre-determined. Many times before, my interest in the peculiarities of the environment in which my childhood was spent had been aroused. The problems of the people who had lost direct contact with the old culture before entirely assimilating the new are numerous and frequently complicate even the simplest phases of their daily lives.

The worldwide conflicts during this generation have, by disrupting the old civilizations, made more urgent the necessity of developing cultural independence in the newer, more heterogeneous lands. It is my contention that, in the case of the Americans of German extraction, this need is the more intense because of the inacceptability of the current ideology of their ancestral country.

Though the characters and situations of these stories are fictionalized, they are attempts to picture life in a small German-American community in a manner which will convey the essence of, rather than the historical truth about, the twenty-five-year period between the conclusions of the two world wars.

For the critical and informational assistance which they have given me, I wish to express my sincere appreciation to Dr. Mody C. Boatright, Mr. Joseph Abrahams, and my mother, Mrs. Max A. Altgelt, without whom my work would have been greatly impeded if not impossible.

Minetta Altgelt
The University of Texas
August 1946

Acknowledgments

Josephine Schulze Miller, my late wife's darling niece, while visiting me during the Christmas holidays in 1994, asked to see whatever her aunt had written about New Braunfels. I dug out the copy of Minetta's master's thesis from nearly fifty years ago. Josi was delighted with the work. That got the ball rolling, and Josi has my eternal thanks.

I want to thank Franz Coreth of New Braunfels and Vienna for his lifelong devotion to my wife—they called themselves "double first cousins"—and, subsequently, to me, for having inspired in the author the character Karl, and for his having helped throughout this effort with

German translations, especially his lovely rendering of the Fontane poem.

I want to thank Judy Alter, to whom I am infinitely grateful for the fine editorial work she has done.

But the one I must give my most special thanks to is Jo Lacy, long in charge of children's literature in the Department of English at the University of Texas at Arlington. For many years Jo had been an avid admirer of my wife's writing. When she read these stories, she begged my permission to create handmade books of the manuscript for me and a few close relatives. These beautiful books are collectors' items.

But Jo did not stop there. She insisted that I submit the manuscript to a university press. A fifty-year-old master's thesis? Such works are generally filed away in the granting institution's library, never again to see the light of day.

Jo would not give up. So I wrote to Judy at the TCU Press, who was familiar with some of Minetta's later writings.

This book, dearest Jo, is here today largely because of your having kept the faith with the memory of my wife and her talents. I simply can't thank you enough.

And, finally, my most profound gratitude to whatever gods may be that I retain such keen memories of the time these stories were written—the time of our courtship—and of all those hopes and dreams, quite a few of which—first and foremost, the birth of our beloved son Roderick, Rick—came true during the nearly forty-six years I was privileged to share the life of the remarkable young woman who created this work.

A. V. Goyne
Arlington, Texas
1996

American Letter
Archibald MacLeish

This, this is our land, this is our people,
This that is neither a land nor a race. We
    must reap
The wind here in the grass for our soul's
    harvest:
Here we must eat our salt or our bones
    starve.
Here we must live or live only as shadows.
This is our race, we that have none, that
    have had
Neither the old walls nor the voices around
    us,
This is our land, this is our ancient ground, —
The raw earth, the wind, and the heart's
    change.
These we will not leave though the old call
    us.
This is our country-earth, our blood, our
    kind.

Kaffeeklatsch
1921

I wonder what is keeping them?" Hedwig Kreutz said impatiently to her husband as she rose once more and looked down the hill in the direction of town.

"They'll be here in a few minutes," Otto said, rocking calmly back and forth in his chair. "The clock hasn't struck yet, and the Kränzchen almost never gets here before four."

Kränzchen was what the older women of the town called their little circle of friends who gathered once every two weeks at the home of one of the group. Although Hedwig knew that her house was in flawless order and almost antiseptically clean, she felt vaguely uneasy about being the hostess. Otto refrained from commenting on her restless-

1

ness, knowing that that would merely agitate her further. In her mind Hedwig was re-checking every room of the house. She had put her best crocheted spread on the guest-room bed where the ladies would leave their things. The pile of magazines and newspapers that Otto always kept to read in the bathroom she had hidden away in a closet. There were fresh guest towels on the racks, and the fixtures had all been scrubbed. The table was laid, and the refreshments were all in the kitchen, covered with cloths and placed over pans of water to keep the dust and ants off. The whole household was waiting for the guests to arrive. Suddenly Hedwig saw an automobile coming up the road, followed, out of range of the cloud of dust it raised, by a carriage.

"Here they come!" Hedwig exclaimed, going toward the door, though she knew it would be several minutes before the vehicles would reach the crest of the hill. After nearly forty years of being married to her, Otto still found Hedwig's occasional spells of nervousness puzzling. For several days she had been cleaning and washing and baking, and everything for the party was so perfectly prepared that he could see no reason for her to worry. In an emergency Hedwig was composed and efficient, but when she faced some event which had been planned in every detail, she seemed almost panicky.

Finally the car stopped before the house, and the host and hostess went out to meet the ladies. A very tall, very black negro in a chauffeur's uniform got out and held the doors open for his mistress and her companions. Although the women bore no physical resemblance to one another, their clothes were of the same tasteful but extremely plain type which only those who are immune to the frivolities of fashion dare to wear. Otto greeted the ladies cordially but formally, whereas Hedwig called all by their given names.

Almost immediately Lilie Schönfeld excused herself, saying, "I'll be back shortly. I just want to go over to see Frieda for a minute."

"Poor Lilie," Elsa Fink said when Frau Schönfeld had disappeared around the corner of the house, "she just can't realize that her daughter is grown up and married."

"It isn't easy to get used to letting them live their own lives," Hedwig explained. "When Martin and Frieda first married I had a hard time keeping myself from telling her how he liked his eggs fried and his shirts ironed."

"What do you think of my new Buick, Herr Kreutz?" Frau Wagner asked. Having no children of her own this talk bored her, and besides she wanted to draw Otto into the conversation.

"Very fine," Otto answered. "If I weren't getting so old I think I'd like learning to operate one. But, as it is, I'll leave that to young people like yourself, Frau Wagner." Otto's gallantry was completely unstrained, but nevertheless it had a subtle quality of mockery in it. This escaped Marie Wagner, who giggled delightedly. She thoroughly loved to be flattered!

"But I don't drive, Herr Kreutz. I feel that only a man can competently handle such a powerful machine." Though she was nearly sixty, Frau Wagner was still undeniably though harmlessly and respectably coquettish.

The conversation was interrupted by the arrival of the other guests. Gustav Bracht helped his wife to alight from the front seat of the carriage, but the two other ladies were left to get out unassisted. When all the group had exchanged greetings, the two men withdrew, and the negro chauffeur drove back to town. Hedwig escorted the ladies into her parlor, where each of the women took a chair after depositing her hat and purse in the guest room. Only then did Hedwig really relax.

"When did you come down from Friedrichsburg, Susanne?" Fräulein Fink inquired of Frau Lauer.

"Oh, I left home almost a week ago," Susanne Lauer answered, "but I spent two days in San Antonio buying some spring clothes."

"Aren't the styles terrible this year?" Auguste Kreutz injected, her face registering shock. "They say that skirts are even shorter than they were last year."

"I've always tried to be fashionable, within reason, but I refuse to expose my ankles!" Frau Bracht said vehemently.

"Oh, you'll do just like the rest!" Marie Wagner insisted. She was the only one of the group who paid much attention to the fashion plates. "You won't want to be thought eccentric, Luise."

"That's what we all told you when you said you would never take part in a public election, Marie," Elsa Fink protested, "and I don't think you have changed your mind, have you?"

"No, I haven't, and I never shall!" Frau Wagner declared. "Men get so *vulgar* at the polls that I don't want to be there."

"Nonsense!" Charlotte Gross exclaimed. "Since women have had the vote, men have begun to show them more respect, even at the polls."

Marie Wagner considered the remark as challenging as if a glove had been flung at her feet. Charlotte Gross had been born and educated in Europe and had had a teaching career before her marriage. She was an ardent feminist, and Marie Wagner had no use for emancipated women. The rivalry between Frau Wagner and Frau Gross was one of the town's greatest assets. If one endowed the public library, the other immediately would subsidize the beautification of the town square. Marie was the daughter of one of the town's most prominent founders, Charlotte, the wife of one of its two important industrialists. Neither felt it necessary to parade her wealth before the public eye, but each was determined to be immortalized as *the* civic bene-factress. Fortunately Charlotte and Marie were not given a chance to debate the merits and demerits of the nineteenth amendment, because just then Lilie Schönfeld came in, and attention was focused upon her.

Seeing that all her guests were comfortable, Hedwig left the room to carry the refreshments to the table.

"How is Frieda getting along, Lilie?" Susanne asked.

"Just fine," Lilie answered. "She is sewing the dress she is going to wear for the Jubilee. When Emmy Dietert discov-ered she was going to have a baby, the committee asked Frieda to replace her as soprano soloist in the Jubilee pageant. Of course, Emmy doesn't want it known that she is expecting, although heaven knows some young women are brazen about having babies these days."

"Yes, isn't it dreadful!" Luise Bracht agreed. "Why, last week I saw Lina Wendlein at Helene Caldwell's wedding, and she was big as a house! Imagine, at a wedding! With dozens of people there!"

"Who is Helene Caldwell?" Susanne Lauer asked curi-ously.

"That's right. You moved away before Tom Caldwell came here with the railroad," Elsa Fink explained. "He mar-ried Dora Heinemann; you remember her. Her father used to have a livery stable on Hill Street. Helene is their child."

"Of course," Susanne recalled. "Didn't I hear that one of the Heinemann boys was killed in the war?"

"Yes," Auguste Kreutz sighed. "That was Dora's nephew. He and my Hermann were at the front together." Auguste rarely entered the conversation, because she was quite hard of hearing and consequently afraid that she might speak too loudly. There was something almost ethereal about the tall old woman dressed entirely in black, her face framed by the fluffy white hair which looked like spun glass. When she spoke in that breathy, monotonously pitched voice of hers, the ghost-like impression was startling.

Hedwig came to the door to announce that the refreshments were ready, and the ladies filed into the dining room. Auguste Kreutz was seated at the foot of the table so that her deafness would be as undisturbing as possible. Each of the other guests settled herself into the most easily accessible chair. From her place at the head of the table, Hedwig surveyed the scene with complete satisfaction. She was justifiably proud of her talents as a hostess, and the guests acknowledged her excellence, first by complimenting her lavishly upon the appearance of her table, then by giving tribute to the tastiness of her cakes and sandwiches.

"Where did you get these wonderful linens, Hedwig?" Marie Wagner asked.

"Otto's mother brought them with her from Europe, and when the old Kreutz household broke up after her death, each of the children got part of the things. It's very, very old, but the quality is so good that I'm always pleased to have occasion to use it."

"Yes, Joachim and I got some beautiful things too which Grossmutter Kreutz left us, but we don't entertain very often these days," Auguste Kreutz said sadly.

"Things were made better in the old days, I think," Charlotte Gross said. "In Europe we girls always had a large supply of linens for our trousseaus, and we made sure they were good enough to last at least one lifetime."

"Your cake is delicious!" Elsa Fink commented. "I certainly want the recipe. Or is it a secret?"

"Oh, no. I'll be glad to give it to you," Hedwig offered graciously. "You sift two cups of flour, and . . ."

"Goodness, do you mean to say you know those complicated proportions by memory?" Elsa asked in amazement. "Living alone the way I do, I bake so seldom I can hardly remember the simplest recipes from one time to the next."

"I notice your roses are as perfect as usual, Hedwig," Susanne said, looking at the centerpiece of large pink blossoms in a shallow cut-glass bowl.

"It's really just because our soil is so good up here on the hill," Hedwig modestly declared. "I haven't nearly as much time to give to my flower garden as I should like."

Everyone else ate with great enjoyment and appetite. Only Lilie Schönfeld declined to drink a second cup of coffee.

"I simply cannot drink more than one cup of it in the afternoon," she complained. "It makes me so nervous that I stay awake half the night." Every significant word Lilie spoke was accented with fluttery little movements of her head and hands. She looked very much like a marionette with an animated face.

"Really, Lilie," Charlotte Gross suggested when the ladies left the table and went back to the parlor, "you ought to go see Dr. Thomson, who just set up offices in the Kreussler Building. He is a chiropractor and gives treatments which he says adjust the spine to relieve nervousness. I've been going to him, and it's marvelous the way my digestion has improved."

"I don't have the vaguest idea what a chiropractor is, Charlotte, and besides I haven't been to a doctor since Frieda was born," Lilie asserted with a superior air. "What is more, I'm not sick. I think some people are just naturally nervous and sensitive the way I am."

"Talented people so often are high strung," Hedwig injected, hoping tactfully to divert the conversation. "Are you going to take part in the concert for the Jubilee, Lilie?"

"Oh, yes," Frau Schönfeld replied excitedly. "Ernst Weisz and I practice together every day for our parts in a piece for two violins with symphonic accompaniment which the orchestra is preparing. He has the *first* violin part, of course." There was no jealousy in the tone of the last statement, only pitiable resignation.

"I had a letter this morning from my cousin, Gretchen Meyer, who lives in California," Marie Wagner suddenly remembered. "She is coming all that way to spend the days of the celebration with us. Just like she says, after all, it isn't every day a town has a seventy-fifth anniversary."

"It looks as if the Jubilee is going to be a very big affair," Elsa Fink said. "Almost every house in town has at least one guest."

"Some of the people who used to live here and are planning to come for the occasion will certainly find things changed," Auguste Kreutz sighed.

"That's very true," Susanne Lauer agreed. "I notice it even when I come back every year for a visit. I guess the war had a lot to do with it."

"It makes one a little sad to feel not quite at home even among the people and places one knows best," Lilie Schönfeld reflected. All but Lilie were working at pieces of handwork which they had brought. While the others talked on, almost unconscious of the rhythmic activity of their hands, Lilie twisted her damp white handkerchief around her long, bony fingers, fingers more familiar by far with the strings of a violin than with a needle and thread. Lilie felt more keenly than she usually did that she was cut off from these other women, who seemed to have so much in common.

It is not rare for women to feel such loneliness, even among old friends. Subconsciously almost every woman traces the feeling to some difference between herself and her associates. Lilie decided that in her own case it was because of her lack of interest in housekeeping and the

domestic arts, a rather unusual state among women of German stock. Elsa Fink felt she was "different" because she was the only spinster in the group, and Marie Wagner, deep inside herself, was convinced the other women thought her not quite their equal because she and her husband had no children. Charlotte Gross and Susanne Lauer thought of themselves as "outsiders" to a degree, Susanne because she had moved away from the little town more than thirty years earlier, Charlotte because she was the only one of the group who was foreign born. Especially when, as now, she was a guest in the home of her successful brother-in-law, Auguste Kreutz felt that her husband's financial reverses constituted a barrier between herself and her old friends. And Hedwig Kreutz could never forget she was the only one of the little clique who lived in the country. Only Luise Bracht did not try to find a scapegoat for her feelings of isolation. Rightly, she took for granted that it was just another manifestation of the greatest human desire: to attain the perfect balance between being like and being unlike others. Luise liked to puzzle out the problems of human behavior and emotions. She read everything she could, both factual and fictional, which concerned people and the workings of their minds.

"Have any of you ladies read that new novel by Sinclair Lewis?" she asked eagerly, hoping she would be encouraged to discuss the book. "It's called *Main Street*," she went on without being solicited, "and concerns a girl who goes to live in a very dull little town. The author makes you feel just as though *you* had lived in a town like that, where nothing exciting ever happens."

At this last remark Gustav Bracht and Otto Kreutz, who had returned just in time to overhear Luise's critique of the book, exchanged an amused glance.

"Well, are you ladies about ready to go?" Gustav asked,

looking at his pocket watch. "It's almost six, and I know that some of you have to be at the meeting tonight to plan the floats for the Jubilee parade."

"My goodness! I had no idea it was so late," Elsa Fink said, jumping to her feet and letting the ball of yarn roll from her lap onto the floor.

Charlotte Gross retrieved the unraveled white woolen thread. Brushing invisible dust off it, she said, "Isn't it difficult to keep a house clean in this dry climate!"

Knowing she had mopped and dusted the entire house thoroughly just that morning, Hedwig struggled to keep her face serene in spite of Charlotte's pseudo-sympathetic comment. How could Charlotte Gross presume to say such things, when Hedwig had once seen her replace an unsoiled but used saucer in the cupboard without washing it first!

"Here comes Furness with the car," Marie Wagner said as she peered anxiously out the window.

All the ladies went into the guest room, put on their hats before the long gilt-framed mirror, and anchored them firmly with dangerous looking hat pins. Carefully, each made sure she had everything she had brought with her and then tried to think of some new way to tell Hedwig how nice the afternoon had been.

Finally the automobile and the carriage rumbled down the hill, and Otto and Hedwig turned to go inside.

"Any coffee and sandwiches left?" Otto asked. "I could make a meal out of a few sandwiches and some of your cake and cookies."

"I thought I'd heat some soup and ask Frieda and Martin to come over and have a light supper with us," Hedwig suggested.

"That would be nice," Otto said as he examined the bundle of crocheted lace which Hedwig had placed on the porch chair. "Na, Alte—*Well, Old Girl*—I'm afraid you are going to have to rip all the stitches you made this afternoon," he teased.

Amused and a bit embarrassed, Hedwig nodded in agreement. "We talked so much that I couldn't concentrate on the pattern. I really ought to know by now that it is useless to try to do anything that requires attention at a *Kaffeeklatsch*."

The Scion

1921

Hedwig Kreutz drowsily stretched her arm out beyond the edge of the bed and groped about the surface of the little night-table until she found her spectacles. Then, with a little grunt, she raised herself to a sitting position in which she could see the clock on the dresser.

"Um Himmels Willen!—*For heaven's sake!*" she gasped. "Es ist ja schon sieben Uhr!—*It is already seven o'clock!*" Seven o'clock, and she had planned to get up especially early this morning to have enough time to do her chores before her son, Martin, left for town. Two weeks before, his wife, Frieda, had gone to her parents' to have her baby, and yesterday the doctor had said it would be all right for Martin to bring them home.

All births in the family were considered joyous occasions, but this one was paramount, because the baby was a boy and the first of his generation to bear the name of Kreutz.

Glancing over toward the bed at the other side of the room, Hedwig saw with relief that her husband was still sound asleep. He had not been well recently, and since their son now managed most of the affairs of the ranch, the old gentleman remained in bed much longer than had formerly been his habit.

Hedwig changed quietly from her voluminous white flannel nightgown into a house-dress and, with the skill of long practice, coiled the heavy mass of gray hair into a huge bun on top of her head. Even in the simple clothing she wore about the house, she had quite an impressive appearance, with her prominent, regular features and tall, stout figure. Nothing but the faded color of her hair betrayed her age, for she was physically vigorous, and an active, outdoor existence had preserved the freshness of her complexion.

With efficient ease she began to prepare a gigantic breakfast for herself and Martin, who lived close by. The two houses in which the Kreutzes lived were built on a hill from which one could look down into the town a couple of miles away. There was an aloofness about the hill, isolated as it was from the world of other people by the two thousand acres of ranch land surrounding it, which had attracted Otto Kreutz. He had bought the place shortly after the birth of his oldest child, Amalie, and the family had lived there ever since. Though the houses which he had had built for himself and his son were substantial and comfortable rather than luxurious, there was much about the entire setting which suggested a European manor or a large feudal estate, a picture which the presence of its owner made more complete.

Otto Kreutz had been born almost immediately after his family had come to Texas from their native Austria. His father, like many of the early settlers of the region, had discarded his noble title and many of the customs of his class, but even in the days of the greatest economic adversity he had never ceased to uphold the traditions of gracious living and *noblesse oblige* in which he had grown to maturity. Otto, though more practical and informal than his father, had acquired many of his social attitudes. At a rather advanced age, after returning from a visit in Europe with relatives, he had married Hedwig, who was also the child of German immigrant ranchers and was twenty years his junior. Together they had accumulated a considerable amount of land and a good herd of cattle and had reared a family of three children, Amalie, Anna, and Martin.

As Hedwig set the table for breakfast she could hear Martin and one of the hired men bringing the buckets of milk onto the cool back porch of the house. After a few moments her son came in and, after kissing his mother on the cheek, sat down with her to eat.

"I hope I didn't track up your floor when I came in," he said, speaking German as all the members of the family preferred to do. "There was a lot of mud in the pens, and I couldn't get it all off my boots."

"Never mind," his mother answered. "I have to mop the dining room floor anyway this morning." The family always ate in the dining room, never in the kitchen, because Otto did not approve saving the niceties of life for special occasions. "At what time do you plan to go to fetch your family?"

Martin smiled shyly to himself. He was not quite accustomed yet to being a father, and any reference to his new status gave him a strange feeling, part pride, part fear, part incredulity. "I guess I'll go about ten-thirty. That way we'll be back here in plenty of time for dinner."

"If I were you," Hedwig suggested, "I'd telephone Frieda before you leave here so that she will know when to expect you. Otherwise she might get excited, and that would not be good for her or the baby."

"Mama," Martin asked suddenly with a worried expression clouding his face, "are you sure two weeks isn't too soon for me to bring Frieda and the baby out here? In town the doctor can see them every day and can be called if he is needed. I can't be at home very much during the day, and you have your own house to take care of."

"Martin, Martin," Hedwig laughed and shook her head from side to side. "Frieda isn't the first woman to have both a baby and a household to take care of. When I was her age I had Amalie and Anna to get off to school every morning and you to watch every minute of the day. We didn't have half the conveniences we have now to make housekeeping easier. Eight days after you were born I was up and about, cleaning, churning, and getting three meals a day for the family. Besides, Frieda and you can eat with Papa and me until she feels strong enough to do all her own chores again. And if a doctor is needed, we can telephone and he will be here within a half hour."

"I guess one always worries most about the first child," the young man sighed as he poured himself a second cup of coffee.

"You can't be more concerned than your father and I," Hedwig replied. "We are going to have to be careful not to spoil little Otto Karl Kreutz."

"I'm very glad Frieda consented to giving that name to the baby," Martin said. "The family tree shows there has been an Otto Kreutz every second generation in a direct line since the twelfth century, and I didn't want to break the tradition. But just to prevent confusion, I think we'll probably make a habit of calling him by his middle name, Karl."

Hedwig felt a sort of tender amusement at Martin's discussion of his son and heir. Her husband had been the same way, and his father before him probably. The Kreutzes had a great pride in the family name, not the kind of vanity which makes one rest on the ancestral laurels, but the sort that makes each generation want to fulfill the promise of the preceding one. As if having shared her thoughts, Martin spoke.

"I had better get back to work now. I don't want Papa to think I'm not interested in keeping his place in good shape."

After Martin had gone, Hedwig cleared away the dishes they had used and put the coffeepot back on the stove. Then, taking the broom from the closet, she started to sweep the long, L-shaped porch which extended along the entire south and east sides of the house. Next she strained the milk and put most of it in jars which she placed into the enormous icebox on the porch. The rest of the milk she put into a container on the kitchen stove to sour for making cottage cheese.

The house still cast its protective shadow as she went out into the little flower garden in front of the porch. It was a little too early in the season for most of the plants to be blooming, but there were buds on the roses which by afternoon would be ready to pluck. The garden had a verdancy and natural lack of organization which gave it an inviting charm surpassing that of more formal landscaping. Like everything connected with the Kreutzes, it was *gemütlich—cozy and comfortable*—to the extreme.

When Hedwig went back indoors, Otto was stirring about in their bedroom.

"Have you found everything you need?" his wife called.

"Don't I always?" Otto answered good-naturedly.

Through the open door the old couple looked at one another with the gentle pleasure of one who sees his own reflection in a mirror. Not that Otto and Hedwig Kreutz were alike or even similar, but each knew the other so well that the element of surprise was entirely gone from their relationship.

Otto Kreutz was a very tall, slender man. As he tried to button the top button of his collarless shirt, he had to bend his knees to see his hands in the mirror which hung above the dresser. Just as he had done hundreds of times before, he finally gave up trying and went over to his wife.

"Da, Alter—*There, Old Boy*," she said as she accomplished what his stiffening hands could not. Tenderly the old man put his arm around his wife's shoulder, and they went into the dining room together.

While Hedwig heated the coffee and prepared his breakfast, Otto looked out the window which opened onto the porch. From the distance he could hear the cattle lowing as Martin let them into the field to graze. Now and then he would hear sheep in the pasture bleating. It was spring, and Otto longed to be out on his horse riding over his land. He hated not being able to exert himself. Not that he was exactly idle, for he did most of the bookkeeping for the ranch. Also he spent a lot of time reading, now that he was required to sit around most of every day. All in all, it was a pleasant life, but the knowledge that his leisure was enforced rather than voluntary made Otto enjoy it less than he might have otherwise.

"Come now, Otto," his wife said. "Eat your breakfast while it is still warm."

Together they sat down at the table. Hedwig knew how much Otto hated to eat alone, and although she had a great deal of work to do, she took time to drink another cup of coffee while conversing with him.

"I wonder where Martin is staying with the mail," Otto said. "I've rather expected to hear from Franziska again. When was it that we last sent her a package?"

"Oh, I believe it was about six weeks ago," Hedwig recalled. "The papers said yesterday that the American Red Cross is beginning to get more relief to the Austrians now, so I suppose we will be having better news before long."

"Poor Franziska," Otto sighed. "I imagine she has regretted many times returning to her home in Europe after Moritz was killed in the Civil War. Moritz was my oldest brother, and I worshipped him. I was terribly jealous of Franziska when they married." Otto smiled as he remembered his childish folly.

"How old are their children now, anyway?" Hedwig asked.

"Let me think," Otto said, stroking his forehead. "The son, Kurt, was nearly grown when I visited Franziska at her home in Innsbruck the year before you and I married. He must be over fifty years old now. His boy fought in France during this last war. The name of Franziska's daughter is Gertrude. She must be a few years younger than Kurt."

"It's quite horrible to think that men of the Kreutz family fought on opposite sides in the war," Hedwig said. "I'll never stop being thankful that Martin didn't have to go overseas."

"I only pray that none of our descendants will ever have to fight in a war," Otto said in a subdued tone.

"Ach, Otto! Let's not even talk about it," Hedwig responded more brusquely than she had intended. She refused even to consider the possibility of there being another war in which her grandsons would have to participate—little Franz Bracht, a gentle, serious child now in his first year of school, and the helpless infant, Otto Karl Kreutz. She smiled faintly. The vision of these youngsters as soldiers was too completely fantastic.

"I'm going to walk down to the mailbox," Otto said when he had finished eating.

"All right, but don't walk too fast," Hedwig urged, "and come right back. It won't be very long before Martin leaves for town. He's bringing Frieda and the baby home, you know."

"Of course, I know," Otto said. "You didn't think I'd forget did you?" Now and then Otto suspected his wife of thinking his memory was failing him in his old days.

Otto took his hat and cane and started down the hill. Hedwig watched him till he reached the barn, then went to make up their beds. Martin had been making up his own ever since Frieda had been away. It was only since his marriage that Martin had shown any signs of trying to spare his mother extra work, Hedwig thought to herself.

The day before, as soon as she had heard when Frieda and the baby would be home, she had gone over to Martin's house and had given it a thorough cleaning. As for her own house, Hedwig decided, she would just dust the parlor and mop the floors of the rooms of the west wing and let it go at that for the day. First, however, she would make her regular morning telephone calls to her two daughters, who lived in town.

Except that Hedwig reported the news that the young mother and child would be home in a couple of hours, the conversations consisted of the usual exchange of trivialities. Elsbeth had lost her first temporary tooth. Wasn't the child a bit too young for that, Amalie asked of her mother. Johanne had taken her first music lesson yesterday afternoon and had been driving the family almost crazy ever since by singing the scales repeatedly. If Franz didn't stop reading so much, he would need glasses in a matter of a few months, Amalie feared. Anna's Toni and Irma were back in school again, after recovering from colds. Irma would have to have her tonsils out during the summer vacation, Dr. Willard had said. Toni and Lucy were going to be in a dance recital soon. They were planning to write invitations to Oma and Opa Kreutz (Hedwig and Otto) and to Tante Amalie and Onkel Fred. There had been a fire in the east end of town the night before. Nothing serious, but hadn't there been a lot of fires lately? There must have been at least three alarms in the last month.

When Hedwig had concluded her telephone chats with her daughters, she began the almost needless task of dusting the living room. Much as she liked the design of her furniture, she realized at times like this how difficult to clean its many carved surfaces and spooled rounds were. As Hedwig polished the glass door of one of the bookcases, she was, as always, tempted to linger over the things which the shelves contained.

There were stacks of family photographs, large and small, old and new. In one pile were documents: birth, marriage, and death certificates; records of honorable discharges from Austrian, United States, and Confederate armies; diplomas of graduation from schools and colleges. On the top shelf lay a scroll tied with a narrow satin ribbon. This, Hedwig knew, was Otto's copy of the family tree. Near it was a little metal stamp with a wooden handle, the seal of the family coat of arms. Beside the stamp, in a velvet- covered etui, the nap of which was worn smooth with age in spots, was the meerschaum pipe which, according to the tradition, at least one man of each generation of Kreutzes must smoke to assure the perpetuation of the family. Though she was not particularly superstitious, Hedwig could never quite regard the pipe without a certain reverence.

After dusting Hedwig propelled the mop over the floors

of the parlor, dining room, and kitchen. The job netted, in addition to some sand, one button which Otto must have lost from one of his suits, a paper-clip, and a small scrap of crocheting yarn. This afternoon she must really try to finish the little cap she was making for Frieda and Martin's baby, Hedwig thought. A few more hours of work on it would be enough.

Martin would be returning from town in a little while, and Otto should be back with the mail. Yes, there he was now. She could hear him whistling as he came up the hill, pausing now and then to get his breath. How well she knew him! When he was in a good mood he whistled "*Muss i' denn,*" and when he was depressed he whistled too, but just a melancholy series of tones in a minor key, not a tune at all, at least none she could identify. Today he was in good spirits, evidently, because as he came into the house he was singing. As he pretended to reach the last tone of the song, Otto playfully swatted Hedwig from behind with the newspaper he had in his hand.

"Geh' nur, du!—*Oh, go on, you!*" Hedwig said chuckling. "Have you no respect for me?"

Having set the vegetables on the stove to cook, Hedwig began to wash the dishes.

"The postman was late today, because his car had a blowout between here and town," Otto explained as he looked through the mail. "Martin passed me on his way to town about a half hour ago. He said they would be back by noon."

"Yes, I know," Hedwig said. "I'll have dinner ready in a little while. Is there any mail for me?"

"Just the *Gartenlaube,*" Otto answered, holding up a magazine he had taken from among the papers he held. "There's the *Zeitung* and a couple of business letters for Martin."

As Hedwig dried the dishes, Otto set the dinner table for four. Suddenly the sound of an automobile was heard outside.

"Are they here already, Otto?" Hedwig called. "Have they come?" Excitedly she dried her hands on her apron and went to the door.

"Ja, Hedie, they are here," the old man answered joyfully as he followed his wife to the porch.

As the old couple reached the front door, Frieda was opening it to let Martin pass through. The cautious way in which the young man held the white bundle in his arms and the finger which Frieda raised to her lips revealed to Otto and Hedwig that the baby was asleep. After Otto and Hedwig had greeted their daughter-in-law warmly, the group went into the parlor. Once inside, Martin took some of the covers off the baby, and the little fellow's reposing face was shown.

"He seems to have grown each time I see him," Hedwig whispered, trying to avoid awakening the child.

"Yes," Frieda agreed. "Everyone seems to think he is an unusually healthy baby." There was a pride in her statement which was of a far more universal sort than the kind of pride which Martin felt in being the father of a son and heir.

Meanwhile, Otto had opened the family Bible, which lay on the library table by the window. Dipping his pen into the open ink-well, he wrote in a flourishing handwriting:

Otto Karl Kreutz, geboren am 28. März, 1923, in Neu Braunfels, Texas. Sohn von Martin Joseph und Frieda Schönfeld Kreutz. Jüngster Stammhalter seiner Familie— *Youngest Son and Heir of his Family.*"

And, as if the scratching sound of the pen and the reverent silence of his elders had told him of his responsibilities, Otto Karl Kreutz began to wail lamentably.

The Masterpiece
1927

Amalie Bracht wearily laid the evening paper aside, took the bright new broom from its hook in the pantry, and went out to sweep the leaves from the pathway in front of the house. Ordinarily she used the time during which the breakfast coffee percolated to get this chore done, but today the sun had already made a scorching griddle of the flagstones beneath her feet. Never before had moving about seemed so difficult. Every motion of her arms was restrained by the starched gingham which clung to her moist shoulder blades.

Fewer pecan blossoms were falling now. Looking upward she could see here and there the black branches of the trees through the profusion of slender green leaves. After each forward step, she swept across the tall, gray shadow at her feet again and again, as if trying to erase it from the clean whiteness of the stones. Seeing her own reflection in a mirror gave her the same sensation. Often she would strain her eyes, remembering the beauty of her face and trying to distinguish the features, but was unable to sweep away entirely the veil-like fog which obscured the details and placed a barrier between herself and the rest of the world. It infuriated her, distressed her. She hated the distorted things she saw, knowing that to other eyes they remained beautiful. From time to time she would be almost overwhelmed by the desire to destroy the things themselves; then realizing how irrational the impulse, she wished with terrifying remorse that she herself could dissolve painlessly and without ugliness into oblivion.

Yes, it was repulsion rather than fear that made death so horrible. Being normally of a vivacious, almost gay nature, she had never been able to fix her attention for long on the unpleasant or sorrowful. Although she felt a sincere sympathy for other people, it was the sympathy of a child, adjusting not from profound understanding but rather by a kind of spiritual osmosis to the attitude of those around her. When the atmosphere changed, she would dismiss the mood with astounding rapidity to make room for another.

Her task done, she sat down limply to adjust her eyes to the relative darkness of the indoors. Deliberately she tried to relax, not to think at all. When she closed her eyes, the haze lifted and things appeared in their old familiar beauty. The straight, symmetrical elm tree in front of the house and the dark, lacy shadows its foliage cast on the brilliant green of the lawn in summer. The happy, confident faces of her family as they gathered around a meal she had prepared for them. The deer leaping through the beams cast by the headlights of the family car when late at night she was returning with her children from a visit at her mother's ranch home.

Dozens of such impressions were catalogued in her mind so that she could select one at will and examine it repeatedly. No thought that she might someday perhaps have only her *memories* of the visible world had caused her to keep this mental file. Always she had felt that she could paint, but she had postponed this like so many other activities until "after the children get old enough to take care of themselves." In her world there were no inanimate things. She approached life with an almost pagan sensualism which empowered her to feel texture with her eyes and color with her heart. But her days were so full with sensing the infinite little miracles that no time remained for her to transpose them onto canvas for others to share. Thus far she had not progressed beyond the painting of a china dinner set which she had begun in her girlhood and which was still unfinished. Even her family of six could not be adequately served with it, so she would place the one plain white cup and saucer by her own plate as a kind of self-admonition for her neglect. It was a standard joke with the family that Amalie had told Fred every Sunday for sixteen years that *soon* she would paint the cup and saucer. Twelve-year-old Johanne delighted in teasing her mother with, "Perhaps you will finish the set in time to give it to me when I marry." And Amalie would affectionately pretend to lay the blame at the feet of her children who had somehow always found something more urgent for her to do. Since the moment she had decided to marry Fred so that she could go back to Mexico with him, each evening had found her with half her plans unaccomplished and left over to fill the next day to twice its capacity.

On opening her eyes she discovered she could actually

see more clearly. If only Dr. Murray were wrong! But she discarded the hope, knowing well its futility. He had given her two alternatives, but the decision must be made soon. Time seemed always to imprison her. She could submit to surgery which would either be fatal or effect a complete cure, or she could resign herself to permanent blindness which would overtake her in a few years. She had hoped that this, like so many of her problems, would solve itself, that something would happen to make one course clearly preferable. Death coming at any point in one's life, she supposed, would find one unprepared. There was so much that needed doing, so much that only she could do.

Self-sufficient though he appeared to be, Fred would be lost without her. Only the quiet orderliness of the home she had made for him prevented his high-strung temperament from making him physically ill. Johanne, now twelve, was rapidly approaching that period of her life, when nothing can lend such stability as a wise and companionable mother. Already Amalie had initiated her in some of the simpler phases of housekeeping, but that is a lesser part of the education for womanhood which only circumstance can occasion. Ten-year-old Franz was already one of those sober, reclusive children who never seem to need anyone but who really rely more than others on parental understanding. Little Elsbeth, a diminutive copy of her mother, was in her first year at school and constituted the family's inexhaustible source of amusement with her ingenuous sagacity and sprightliness. Who but Amalie would answer her unquenchable "whys"? The baby, Annalies, not yet two, was still devoid of any distinguishing characteristics except an unmistakable facility for asserting herself.

Just now, an explosive syllable summoned Amalie into the nursery to furnish the attention so audibly demanded. Raising the child from the play pen onto the floor Amalie offered her hand as support to the tottering little figure, but the child, clutching both its tiny hands to its chest and vehemently screeching a series of negative sounds, ran through the doorway hoping to escape restraint. From previous observation Amalie knew the next step in the little one's adventure. She stood back, watching the child approach the screen door which opened onto the porch. The baby struggled to push it open, trying to rush through before it banged shut again. Several times the door would yield a few inches, only to be pulled back by the spring. Instinctively, Amalie went to hold the door open long enough for the round little body to walk through, but the child turned on her and beat her thighs, resentful of the assistance which had been offered. Then with a sudden bound the little palms hit the obstructing door, flung it wide open, and triumphantly ran outside, leaving the door to slam noisily shut.

Smiling a bit sadly, Amalie followed the child out onto the porch. The human inpulse for emancipation must be inherent, she concluded. Something inside each of us demands expression, and none is really satisfied until he has found some symbol to outlast and represent him. In each of us one sense predominates, and Amalie Bracht *saw* life. Considered in that light, blindness took on a hideous finality which even death could not duplicate.

Closing the door behind her, she found the keyhole with one hand while she inserted the key with the other. It occurred to her that she must have dozens of such little invariable patterns for performing ordinary acts, patterns which because of the element of habit involved had kept her from becoming aware that her eyesight was failing long after the acuity of her vision had begun to diminish. Subconsciously her mind had taken over, without warning, the task of protecting her by increasing the delicacy of her other senses. She realized for the first time that she knew the relative position of almost everything in the house and the neighborhood, how many steps before turning into the neighbors' yard, how many steps to take before reaching the garden gate. Taking the child by the hand, she walked across the street and up the steps of the neighbors' veranda.

When Helen MacMillan opened the door in response to the sound of the bell, she knew immediately that the woman before her was troubled. After a heap of wooden blocks had been provided to keep the baby busy, Helen settled herself and her guest in two of the large, brocaded easy chairs which gave her parlor an inviting, comfortable look.

"What is it, Amalie?" she asked, coming as always directly to the point. "Something has obviously been keeping you awake nights. You never could lose sleep without looking like an owl for days afterward," she continued, trying to give her voice its usual brusque quality.

She had known the Bracht family since her husband had brought her to the little Texas town nearly ten years ago. He was their family doctor, she their confidante. Before her marriage to Roy MacMillan she had been a pediatric nurse in the large midwestern hospital where he had been an intern. Having no children of her own, she had befriended every youngster in the neighborhood. There was little in her rather hard, masculine manner to suggest her great gentleness and deeply affectionate nature, but every detail of her household showed the efforts she had exerted in trying to make it a place which would make children feel welcome.

"Helen," Amalie began hesitantly, "I've gone to another doctor."

"No need for apology," her companion answered with forced flippancy. "Roy hasn't got the market cornered."

"Dr. Murray is an oculist," Amalie said quietly, watching the change of expression on her friend's face. "He says I have a brain tumor which will blind me unless I have it removed almost immediately. An operation would either kill or cure."

Countless times Helen MacMillan had given faith to children whose futures were limited to one revolution of the hands of the clock or whose horizons would always be restricted to the dimensions of the hospital bed. In despondent parents she had instilled the courage to spend years making tolerable a small life which they had brought into existence. But what was one to say to a woman whose decision would determine the lives of five besides herself?

"The children need me so," Amalie said when her friend showed no signs of answering. "I could go on for a few years like this, and they would be almost old enough to take care of themselves before . . . ." She could not bring herself to finish her statement.

"Have you told Fred?" Helen finally asked.

"Of course he knows I have been to Dr. Murray, but he doesn't know how serious it is. And I don't want to tell him until I decide what to do." The pained attitude of her face grew more intense. "I'm not ready, Helen. I"ll never be ready. I want to see the first suggestion of a beard on my son's cheeks. I want to read in the papers that the bride's mother, Mrs. Fred Bracht, looked charming in her blue lace gown. I want to paint the pictures I have dreamed. I shall never be ready!" The voice which had been growing more impassioned broke suddenly.

Helen MacMillan laid a large comforting hand on the bowed shoulders. The baby, noticing its mother's weeping, wailed pitiably, not knowing why. Putting aside her own grief, Amalie rose to quiet the child.

"It's all right, Helen," she said with strained composure. "I know I must decide for myself."

Outside once again, she squinted at the brightness of the

sun. What would it be like not to be able to see at all, she wondered and closed her eyes. It was strange to discover how little the sureness of her steps was impaired as she walked down the familiar path. From the church nearby the angelus was ringing out resoundingly. The high-pitched chirping of crickets filled the sultry air. As they reached the curb, Amalie felt the child at her side stop suddenly. Just in time she saw an old car full of high school youngsters race past without regard for the safety of pedestrians. The noise of the motor had been drowned out by the sound of the bells, and lost in thought, she would not have noticed the speeding automobile until it was almost upon them. With horrible clarity the realization came to her. The baby had been leading her, had unwittingly perhaps saved both their lives. Dazed by retrospective fear, she managed to get across the street.

The older children were busy with their evening chores when she and Annalies entered the dusky coolness of the large, brick house. Amalie glanced at the clock and without registering any reaction, began to set the table for supper. The episode of the automobile still gnawed at her mind. Had it been due to inattention or to the impairment of her sight? Reaching to the top shelf of the cupboard, she took down the hand-painted dinner set, until now reserved for Sundays and holidays, and laid places for six. When the plates and silver had been neatly arranged she went back for the cups and silver. With a tenderness she struggled to hide even from herself, she took the plain white cup and saucer from their places and started for the dining room.

Just as she reached across the table, she heard the gravel on the driveway grind under the wheels of Fred's Model-T. Her hand began to tremble uncontrollably and the cup and saucer crashed to the floor in a shattered heap. Carefully she picked up the fragments, caressing each shapeless chip and gathered them into her apron to carry away.

Supper was the usual short noisy affair. In large families, mealtime is synonymous with a conversational resume of the day's events, especially when children comprise the majority. Franz gained his father's permission to join the cub Boy Scout troop on an overnight hike to Huaco Springs, while Johanne informed her mother that she would finally have to be allowed to get a long dress, since it had been decided that the recital of her voice class would be "formal." Elsbeth injected frequent questions and her usual numerous naive observations. And the baby lustily punctuated the entire scene with meaningful grunts and cymbalings with her plate and spoon, while the tablecloth and her little blue bib suffered the inevitable consequences. Fred, as was his habit, reserved his report for the later hours, when, after the smaller children had been put to bed and the older ones had retired to their rooms to study, he and Amalie could sit quietly and share their news in relatively uninterrupted peace.

Suddenly Johanne noticed the china. "Why, Mother, you used the Sunday dishes!" she exclaimed incredulously. "Is today anything special?"

Amalie smiled, taking the time to keep her voice from wavering. "I thought I might like to drink from one of the finished cups . . . just this once," she said with mock apology to disguise her feelings.

Unaware of the implication, the children laughed and teased her affectionately. No one had noticed that Amalie had been particularly quiet during the meal. Lately she said very little, partly from preoccupation with her thoughts, but largely because she was afraid of what she might say if she ever allowed herself to begin. She had never indulged her sentimentality, and now she was so often close to tears that she did not dare to speak. She wanted to solve the problem as unemotionally and intelligently as possible, to be able to spare Fred and the children as long as she could the tormenting uncertainty. Without raising her eyes she felt the children staring at her impatiently, waiting for her to excuse them. She looked at them, unable to see their faces clearly through the tears, then at Fred, who stood by the window lighting his pipe, the twilight tinting his face a faint translucent bronze. She traced the profile with her eyes, the smooth, high forehead, the long, narrow nose, the soft, full lips, the beautiful curvature of the firm jaw. Every feature incorporated strength, yet she remembered with a kind of tender amusement how far more upset he had been by the birth of the children or their infrequent illnesses than she. Give us strength to do what must be done, she prayed, more to her own heart than to any outside power. At her nod of dismissal, the children scampered out of the room.

"I am going to have to leave you and the children for a few weeks, Friedrich," she said, trying not to reveal the gravity of the situation.

He turned to face her. "Dr. Murray and I arranged everything as soon as he told me. We've just been waiting for you to decide," he said quietly. Because he was silhouetted against the darkening window, Amalie could not see how deeply moved yet relieved was his expression. It was a moment such as every normal woman longs for. The moment when, after the newness of love is gone, she feels for the first time really secure: completely protected yet altogether free. It is at that moment that she triumphs in the highest art . . . the art of *being*.

"When I get back I am going to paint a picture of the

children," she said. "I'm going to call it *Orpheus and the Three Graces.*"

"Your masterpiece has already been produced, Amalie," he replied, taking her hand. "Painting it will be just a post-script."

Depression
1929

The uniformed man walked leisurely down the aisle, calling out the name of the little town with the peculiarly distorted pronunciation which only railroad conductors can achieve, "Noo Brownsville! Noo Brownsville!" Twice he stopped, collected little white tickets stuck behind the clasps on the window-shades, then continued on to the next car. After emitting a series of asthmatic wheezes, the locomotive jolted to a stop with one long sigh.

Fred Bracht placed his grey homburg rather carelessly on his head and started for the exit. About the middle of the car, his passage was blocked by two nuns assembling their parcels. Two uninterrupted days and nights on trains had worn the man's patience thin, so that the blood vessels at his temples throbbed visibly as he struggled to maintain his composure while the women calmly gathered their equipage.

Once outdoors, Fred Bracht felt that his usual good humor was somewhat fortified by the clean, fresh air of the late summer twilight.

"Where have you been, Fred?" old Joachim Kreutz called as he shifted to his left hand the metal sign with which he was signaling the traffic to stop for the train to pass.

The two men shook hands. "I've just come back from two weeks in the North. I went up there to get some new machinery for the plant. We have had so many contracts with the State Highway Department that we needed more equipment." Fred Bracht had reason to be proud of the success of his business. He had drawn the plans, sold the stock, and supervised the construction, and now, after five years of ceaseless work, the little crushed-stone corporation was paying dividends which exceeded all his expectations. If the profits continued to be good, he planned to take his family to Europe the next summer for a vacation. Next year all the children, even little Annalies, would be old enough to enjoy traveling. And Annalies would like nothing better than meeting her European relatives of whom her father had told her so much. Fred himself had been to parts of Europe but never to Germany or the Scandinavian countries, so the trip would also hold something new for him.

"Yes, business is certainly booming," the older man said. "It reminds me a lot of 1907."

The full implication of Joachim's remark did not impress Fred. He had been living in Mexico at the time of that financial panic and had escaped most of its effects. After bidding the old man good-bye, Fred called for his suitcase at the baggage room and headed down the railroad track in the direction of home.

Amalie Bracht greeted her returning husband at the door with a warm if unexciting kiss, and a "But I didn't think you'd be back so soon!"

"I managed to finish all the business sooner than I had expected," the man explained, "and I was anxious to get home," he added, casting a smiling glance around the room, as if retouching the picture of it which he carried in his mind. All the household, from the sturdy, unmatched furniture to the fresh white tablecloth, reflected and complemented him. Seated at the supper table with his five most treasured responsibilities, Fred Bracht was like the prototype of the Biedermeier tradition. An adventurous youth had preceded his secure maturity, and now, at forty-seven, he was one of the thousands of vigorous, confident heads of small corporations who, in September of 1929, were enjoying a fool's paradise of prosperity.

While everyone helped himself to cottage cheese, molasses, and sausage, the scene was busily silent. Then, suddenly, as if by signal, all of the children burst out simultaneously with the bits of news they had been saving all day to tell. Laughing, Amalie hushed them all with a soft, "One at a time!" By virtue of seniority, Johanne was permitted to give her information first. She had found out from Sister Franciska during her voice lesson today, all about the two new nuns next door. The sixth- and seventh-grade teacher, Sister Veronika, was Irish, middle-aged, and jolly. The first- and second-grade teacher was a young Bavarian girl, who had been in this country only since shortly after the war.

"I can hardly wait to meet Sister Veronika," the young girl continued. "Sister Superior said she makes beautiful lace and embroidery, and maybe she will teach me how."

Elsbeth sat quietly, as if having forgotten what she had been so eager to tell. In a few days she would be enrolling in the Catholic school, because a recent illness had caused her to fall behind her class at public school, and her father had decided that the private tutoring which the nuns could give her would be more effective than placing her in the grade beneath her former classmates. The prospect of having to adjust to a new school and new friends was not pleasant.

"I want to go to school, too," a high voice whined. Little Annalies, just five, felt acutely that she was excluded from much of the family's activity because she was "the baby."

"If you would let me get in a word edgeways, I'd tell you my news," the mother said kindly. "The Sister Superior said she would allow Annalies to go to the kindergarten, if she promised to behave like a young lady." The condition had been entirely of Amalie's invention, but she delivered it with complete sobriety.

"I'll be a lady! I'll be a lady, if it kills me!" the little girl screeched delightedly.

"That I will have to see," Franz said in the resigned tone of voice fourteen-year-old brothers adopt with little sisters. One reproving glance from his parents discouraged his expressing himself further in this manner.

The rest of the supper progressed smoothly, the older members of the family carrying on a lively chatter about the affairs of the day, occasionally punctuated by Annalies' singing dreamily to herself, "I'm going to schoo-ul, I'm going to schoo-ul!" until her mother gently but firmly led her howling to the kitchen and made her stand in the little nook next to the chimney under a cupboard. But indignation cannot long survive in a body well-fed and tired with play, so Annalies soon fell asleep instead of repenting her bad manners.

For the next three months the Bracht family was almost too busy to keep track of time. After a long summer of relaxation, the older children welcomed the familiar routine of the school term, and Annalies was so engrossed in the adventure of learning to form her letters that she could scarcely be persuaded to go out to play. Amalie, unaccustomed to Annalies' absence, invented dozens of little chores to dull her sense of acute loneliness. The crash had come. Fred stayed at the plant from early morning until after dark, then brought his work home with him.

While the local hotels and resorts received many a cancellation, the culverts along the river banks sheltered more than their capacity of migrants of another sort. And the houses of the generous were labeled with blue chalk crosses marked on gate or sidewalk by the hoboes. The neighborhood which had long since become inured to the noise of the nearby railroads became aware again of the train schedule.

Sister Angelica stood at the window of her classroom looking out. Recitations had had to be temporarily stopped, because the windows vibrated so violently while the freight trains passed that hearing anything else was impossible. It had become almost a game with the children to count the people sitting on the flat-cars and standing in the doorways of the big box-cars.

"Thirty-eight this time," Sister Angelica reported as she turned to face her class. It was too near time for dismissal to justify beginning a new lesson. She tapped the little bell on her desk, and the children slid from their seats into the aisles. In droning chorus the treble voices recited the Lord's Prayer, scarcely able to wait for the "amen" to permit them out into the sunlight.

"Give us this day our daily bread . . . ." Memories too dreadful to be invited gained surreptitious entrance into Sister Angelica's mind. Years of undernourishment, interrupted sometimes by a precious box of food from America, even the little spaces between the cylindrical cans filled with loose grains of rice. Finally the German bishop arranged her passage abroad and her acceptance by an American convent, where she could earn her board and keep. It had seemed a small price at the time, considered in that light, she reflected, unconsciously placing a glass weight, in which a small spray of edelweiss was encased, atop the papers on her desk. The school bell rang, and the children eagerly rushed outdoors.

Annalies Bracht squeezed her plump little figure through the space in the picket fence where one broad slat had conveniently disappeared. Home once more, she dumped her books on the seat of the grotesque hatrack in the hall and made straight for the icebox. Having selected a large apple, she went out to the back steps to eat it.

Dry, dead leaves huddled together against the wall wherever the wind had driven them, and here and there, on the clean white gravel, lay the empty brown and green pecan hulls, looking like blossoms not yet full blown. Occasionally, at the rasping sound which introduces the blackbird's call, Annalies would search the thinning foliage of the trees for the source of the intrusive discord. The harsh, ugly sound frightened her, but she was greatly attracted by the glossy feathers of the bird, not really black at all, but opalescent in the sunlight.

Just then the familiar dusty little coupe rattled into the yard to disturb the child's communion with the autumn afternoon. Formerly Annalies would have been greatly pleased to have her father return early from work, but now even she was aware of the change in him as he greeted her tersely and immediately went indoors. Shortly afterward, her mother came out and said in a voice more hushed than was necessary, "You must be very quiet. They blasted out at the quarry today, and papa has a bad headache."

It occurred suddenly to Annalies that not merely her

father had changed recently; lately everyone seemed either to be cross or to have a headache. But her infant mind, unequipped to concentrate long on any problem, abandoned the analysis of adult conduct to crack and eat the pecans which she found lying about her feet.

At the sound of footsteps crunching the gravel behind her, she turned to see a strange little man with a shapeless canvas sack flung over his shoulder, rounding the corner of the house.

"Got any knives for me to sharpen, little lady?" the friendly voice spoke. "Or scissors, for that matter. I'll sharpen all your knives and scissors for a cup of coffee and a sandwich."

"Just a minute, and I'll ask my mother," the little girl said, somewhat startled by the man's sudden appearance. Then remembering her mother's words of a few moments before, she reconsidered. "I'll go get them," she said, disappeared for a few seconds, and returned with her kindergarten scissors and a small drawer full of kitchen implements of various sorts.

"You'll have to be very quiet," she whispered. "Papa has a headache."

"Guess all of us have a headache of one sort or another," the man responded, trying to comply with the little girl's orders. Soon he began to hum quietly to the accompaniment of the whirling grindstone.

The child was greatly fascinated by the sparks flying from the glistening blades of the knives. In the midst of his work, the man took off his battered derby, and Annalies noticed that the hat band had a kind of moiré pattern made by the salt of evaporated perspiration. From time to time he would stop and run the cutting edge of a knife between the cushions of his right thumb and forefinger, then go on working and humming to himself.

"I could work much better and faster if you got me that coffee and a sandwich," the man said after a while, smiling slyly.

Thinking that the man suspected her of falling down on her part of the bargain, the child promptly went into the house. With some difficulty she managed to make him a shapeless cheese sandwich, which she placed on a tray beside the cup of leftover coffee and carried out to her busy companion.

"I'm sorry that I couldn't heat the coffee," she apologized, "but I can't reach the matches." At this moment the screen door banged noisily behind her, and with a gasp she waited for signs which would mean that her father's rest had been disturbed.

As she had feared, she heard Fred Bracht's footsteps first on the stairs, then in the hall, and finally his deep, sonorous voice saying, "Die Mama hat gesagt du solltest still sein, Annalies—*Mama has said you must be quiet.*"

Nothing in his voice betrayed his bad humor, but his calling her "Annalies" instead of the more affectionate "Liesel" gave him away completely. Then he noticed the stranger unconcernedly drinking the coffee which had been placed beside him.

"Who gave you permission to work and eat on my property?" Fred said gruffly, almost completely out of temper from pain and irritation.

"I hear you have a headache," the scissors grinder said, ignoring the other's question.

"I have, and I'll thank you to leave this minute without further molesting this child."

"Headaches seem to be making the rounds these days," the worker continued in his soft, unruffled tone. "Had one myself not long ago, every day from nine to five. Then one day they said they couldn't use me anymore, so I walked out of my cage and haven't had a headache since. I've had cold feet a few times, I guess that's natural at my age, but each time I'd just get up and shake a leg, and everything came out all right." He stopped and took another bite of the sandwich, but Fred Bracht had sat down on the step and was listening intently to what the stranger said and did not take the opportunity of interrupting.

Annalies was incredulous when she heard the man say he had worked in a cage. "Were you a lion tamer?" she asked excitedly.

"No, I stood all day at a grilled window in a bank and took people's money," the stranger continued. "All day long I'd watch their faces as they handed me their savings. Some would bring checks and big rolls of bills, and some would bring bags of nickels and dimes, but none of them looked happy. I used to think it was because they didn't have enough, but I soon found out it was because the next fellow might have more, that they didn't know peace of mind."

The stranger collected his tools and slowly placed them in the sack. "Yessirree," the man continued, "I'll take cold feet any day instead of a headache." And quietly rising, he slung his bundle over one stooped shoulder and walked away.

For a while the father and child sat wordless and pensive in the oppressively sultry twilight.

"There is going to be a norther tonight," the father finally said.

"How do you know, Papa?" the child asked, awed, as always, by her father's meteorological prophesies.

"By that dark wall of clouds in the north, and it's too hot to stay this way," the man answered with the usual pleasure at having taught his child something new.

As if having waited to be announced, the wind began

suddenly to lash the tops of the trees, and the atmosphere was filled with the fragrance of cedar drifting from the hills. Throughout the house doors slammed noisily shut, and Amalie's and Johanne's steps could be heard as they scurried to close the windows. Franz and Elsbeth, who had been visiting in the next block with schoolmates, rushed home to be sheltered from the rapidly falling temperature.

"Let's go in now, Liesel," the father said, placing his strong, bony hand on Annalies' shoulder. "Mama must have supper almost ready by now."

And for the first time in months Fred Bracht relaxed as he laid down the evening paper to exchange a glance with Amalie over the heads of their children as they sat down to a steaming meal.

"Isn't it about time you children were writing to Santa Claus?" he inquired, looking at Annalies with mock solemnity. "You'd better not wait too long. But mind you don't ask for the moon."

What Will People Think?
1938

"Karl, Karl Kreutz!" Miss Rogers called to one of her fifth-grade pupils who sat alone on the steps of the school building.

"Yes, ma'am?" the boy responded as he turned to see who had addressed him.

"Your mother just telephoned and said you need not wait here any longer for your father. He's been delayed, and you're to meet him at your Aunt Anna's house at five-thirty."

"Yes, ma'am," the boy answered, smiling broadly as he rose. Two whole hours in town to do as he pleased!

"Just a minute, Karl," Miss Rogers said. "I want to talk to you before you go."

"Yes, ma'am," the boy sighed. Suddenly the two glorious hours ahead seemed very short, and Miss Rogers was going to take up precious time by lecturing him.

"I'm worried about you, Karl," Miss Rogers was saying. "Your grades are good and you don't make any trouble for me, but why don't you play with the other boys during recess?" Miss Rogers was a kind woman. She did not mean to be blunt, but all subtler means she had used in trying to understand Karl Kreutz had failed.

"I don't like baseball," Karl answered simply.

"But the boys don't always play ball," Miss Rogers continued. "Don't you like to play at all, Karl?"

Karl hung his head. "Kids are silly," he said sullenly. "Why don't people leave me alone?" There was a resentful look in the boy's eyes which warned Miss Rogers that she had better not pursue the investigation any further at the moment.

"All right, Karl," she said, somewhat disheartened as she started to go back indoors. "Don't forget that you're to meet your father at your Aunt Anna's at five-thirty."

"Yes, ma'am," Karl said. He was ashamed to have flared up like that when Miss Rogers was just trying to be helpful. She was really very nice, and he'd have to make it up to her somehow.

As he walked down the hill toward town, Karl could not get his mind off himself and his troubles. Why wasn't he like other eleven-year-old boys? They seemed actually to like getting scratched up and dirty. They acted as if they thought it was wonderful to slide to third base, even if they scuffed their shoes and skinned their knees. The girls weren't so bad. Karl spent more time with them, although usually he would rather be alone just looking on. The other boys made fun of him for that, but at least the girls talked about something besides ball games and movies.

Karl didn't go to many movies. Saturdays, when he was

not in school, the shows were always western thrillers. Cowboys and rodeos didn't have much attraction for Karl. All his life he had lived on a ranch, and he knew that the hired men didn't wear embroidered shirts and fancy boots. Never in his life had he known the cowhands on his father's place to practice rope tricks or sit around an open fire playing guitars and singing "Home on the Range." Ranching was hard work, and it hurt Karl to see his father come home every night, dusty and tired. He would have liked to help his father, but Martin Kreutz always told his son the work was too strenuous for a boy. Instead Karl washed dishes or even marked the hem for his mother occasionally when she sewed herself a dress. But he couldn't tell that to the boys at school. It was bad enough having them think he was a sissy without their knowing he did housework.

That was the big trouble with everything, Karl thought to himself. He got along fine with grown-ups. They praised him for being polite and for learning his lessons. But when he was with the boys at school they made fun of him, because he remembered to say "Thank you" and "Excuse me" at the right times and because he would rather read than play baseball.

Karl liked to read, and often he would sit and just think about the wonderful things he had read about in his Grandfather Kreutz's books. Karl had been too young when his Opa Kreutz died to remember what he had been like, but he had heard others speak of him in admiring terms. Once Frau Wagner had said that Opa Kreutz had been the politest man she had ever known. Opa had been courteous, and he had probably never played baseball in his life, but nobody ever called *him* a sissy. It was different with grown-ups. That was why Karl often pretended he was a man. Men didn't have to use bad grammar or play rough games in order to be considered "regular." But he couldn't fool even himself into thinking he was grown-up for long, because some kid would always mock him and say he was "putting on."

I don't look like a sissy, Karl thought as he looked at himself in the plate-glass store window before which he had stopped. He was tall and well-developed for his age, and there was nothing peculiar about the way he walked or talked. Of course he had a slight German accent, but so did most of the other children he knew. Although Frieda Kreutz always saw to it that her son was nicely dressed, his clothes were never very expensive. He wore sneakers and knickerbockers just like most of the other boys his age.

Not even his face was dainty, Karl decided as he leaned over to examine his features more closely. That was when he saw the vase in the show window. A little table was the main item on display, but it was the vase on the table which caught Karl's eye. It was white porcelain, about six inches tall, and had a brightly-colored nosegay painted on its side. Around its top rim was a narrow gilt band. Just the thing to give Miss Rogers to show her I didn't mean to be cross with her awhile ago, Karl thought.

The proprietor of Levy's Treasure House was a fat little man with sloping shoulders who pointed the toes of his flat feet outward as he approached his young customer.

"What can I do for you, young man?" he asked, clasping his hands and inclining his head forward in such a way that his whole attitude seemed one of servilitude.

"I'd like to buy that vase in the window," Karl said with deliberate casualness, as if he were quite accustomed to purchasing things without first asking their price.

"Yes, sir," Jake Levy said and went to the showcase to get the vase.

While Mr. Levy was wrapping the package Karl looked around the store. It wasn't exactly an ordinary shop, because some of the merchandise was new and some was second-hand. All sorts of furniture lined the walls and clustered in little groups down the middle of the big room. At the back of the store there were shelves of household appliances and clocks and light fixtures of all sizes and styles. Hanging from the ceiling was a dusty crystal chandelier which immediately captured Karl's attention. It was neither large nor elaborate, but to Karl it was one of the most beautiful things he had ever seen. In one of Opa Kreutz's books there was a picture of a ballroom in Schönbrunn Castle in which there were many crystal chandeliers ablaze with candles. People in beautiful costumes were waltzing about on the highly-polished floor, and here and there were huge arched doorways through which one could see other rooms and terraces. When Karl looked at the picture he could almost feel himself spinning around in time to the music of stringed instruments. He liked to dance. Sometimes his mother, who was scarcely taller than he, would put a record on their phonograph and dance him about the parlor. Recently she had taught him to take the man's part and lead their steps around the floor. It made him want to close his eyes and imagine he was his Greatgrandfather Kreutz at a court ball in Vienna. He had done that once, but his mother had scolded him, because he had bumped into a table and broken a lamp.

The cash register rang up the sale, and Karl remembered the little vase.

"That will be seventy-five cents," Mr. Levy was saying.

Karl gulped. Seventy-five cents! It was Thursday, and his weekly allowance of fifty cents was half spent. The Kreutzes didn't charge purchases except at the grocery, and Karl couldn't ask his father for an advance on next week's spending money, because he would have had to explain that he was buying the vase to prove to Miss Rogers that he hadn't meant to be rude to her. That would make Papa angry.

"I only have a quarter," Karl answered shyly. He was terribly embarrassed. He couldn't tell Mr. Levy that he wouldn't take the vase after the man had already wrapped it for him. Besides he was determined to have the gift to take to Miss Rogers the next morning. Suddenly the solution to his problem came to him.

"I could do fifty cents' worth of work for you, Mr. Levy," Karl felt strangely proud as he said the words. He had never worked for money before in his life. Papa didn't believe in paying members of the family for chores they did at home. He provided his wife and son with all they needed and set aside an allowance for each of them and himself. It was not that Martin Kreutz was miserly. The family was moderately wealthy, but Martin didn't believe in extravagance, and he wanted his son to learn the value of the dollar. What better way was there to learn that than to work for pay, Karl thought.

Jake Levy smiled. He managed the store by himself, and he rarely had time to keep it as clean as he would have liked.

"You could wash the show-case window," he said. That was about a fifty-cent job, and it needed doing.

Karl was greatly pleased and could hardly wait for Mr. Levy to get the equipment. Finally the man returned from the back of the store with a little stepladder, some scraps of cloth, and a bucket of water. Then he went back to get a can of scrubbing powder and a pole with a perpendicular strip of rubber on its end, with which he showed Karl how to wipe the water off the plate glass when it had been cleaned.

Immediately Karl went to work on the inside surface of the large window. It was fun moving the soapy cloth over the glass in little circles. It reminded Karl of making the ovals in penmanship class at school, only he enjoyed this more, because he didn't have to worry about staying between two lines. Slowly he began to coat the glass with white clouds so dense that he could scarcely see out to the sidewalk.

A woman stopped before the window. Karl grinned at her, thinking he must look rather funny perched up on the step-ladder in a show-case. The woman looked right at him, but she showed no sign of having seen him. At first Karl was a bit disappointed in her for ignoring him, but then he knew why, and he was suddenly pleased. I can see out, but no one can see in, he thought. It was a rather strange feeling. Karl had always wished he could make himself invisible and watch people without their being aware of his presence. He liked observing people and imagining what they were really like. Somehow he could never quite make himself believe that people acted the same around him as when he was not there with them. Often when he walked into a room where Mama and Papa or Oma and her friends were talking, conversation would stop as if there were something Karl should not hear. Then the grown-ups would pretend great interest in Karl and try to talk with him about school and his friends. His friends! Mama and Papa didn't know that just giving big birthday parties for him didn't win him friends or invitations to other children's parties either.

The woman before the window had walked on, but a man had come into the shop. Even before the stranger started to talk to Mr. Levy, Karl knew he was a mill hand. The workers at the cotton textile mill were different from the town's people or the farmers. They dressed more cheaply than most of the old residents and more casually than the country people when they came to town.

The people from mill town weren't poor. They made

rather good wages and their houses were fairly nice, though they were cheaply constructed. Milltown was the only part of the community where the people didn't keep gardens. One would have supposed that they, even more than other people, would want to get outdoors into the sunshine after working in the constant dampness of the factory. Karl had gone through the textile plant with his social studies class once, and he had thought the big machines and the monotonous activity of the workers terribly depressing. No wonder the mill people all were so pale and tired looking.

The man who had come into the store was going to buy a second-hand upright piano for his daughter, Jeannie, who, he said, was taking lessons. Karl wondered whether this man's daughter was the same Jeannie from Milltown whom his cousin, Toni, had been talking about. Toni had said that Jeannie Kimball had worn a gingham evening dress to the junior-senior prom last month when the other girls had net and taffeta gowns. Lots of girls wore gingham for school, but to a dance! It wasn't until several years later that gingham evening dresses were featured in the fashion magazines, and the girls of the town lost their snobbishness about cotton materials.

The man was arranging to buy the piano on the installment plan. Papa never let any of the family buy anything unless they could afford to pay cash in full. Once he had explained to Karl how the Retail Merchants' Association had records of people's credit ratings and how important it was to maintain a good reputation.

Everything depended on one's reputation, and Karl had always been made to feel that just being a Kreutz obligated him to be above reproach in every way. It wasn't entirely comfortable, being the only son of a family which for many generations had occupied a position of prominence and respect. It gave a disquieting importance to everything,

Karl Kreutz thought as he looked down at the smiling little negro boy who had come into the store and stood close by as Karl descended the ladder to clean the lower portion of the window.

The little black boy was with his mother, whom Karl recognized as Henrietta Mumford, who did his Aunt Amalie's washing. Henrietta was a big negress with a quiet dignity which no one could fail to admire. She was as much a native of the town as anyone could be and was probably one of its best known residents. Oma Kreutz had said that Henrietta's grandparents had been among the very few slaves ever to have been held in the county, and after the Emancipation Proclamation they had asked to stay on as servants of their former owners. Everyone in town knew that Henrietta had been named for old Mrs. Schumann, in whose home she had succeeded her mother as housemaid. Like many of the local negroes, she could speak German, even to the extent of imitating the Nassau dialect spoken by her employer. Yes, even Henrietta had a reputation to uphold, Karl thought, a reputation for dependability and cleanliness. She was as proud of doing a superior job of laundering other people's clothes as Martin Kreutz was of having the best herd of cattle in the county.

Karl had finished cleaning the inside of the window, so he went out to the sidewalk to wash the outer surface of the glass. It wouldn't be long now before he would finish the job and be in possession of the little vase. But it was something else which made the boy whistle gaily as he scrubbed the glass with the soapy solution. As the sun approached the horizon, the window reflected the rosy brilliance of the western sky. There was beauty in the glass, a beauty which it had not had before Karl had begun to polish it. Each time he had washed a small area of the plate-glass, Karl got down from the ladder and stepped back to view his work.

No painter could have been more particular about his work than Karl Kreutz was about this, his first job. It gave him a great sense of accomplishment, greater than making good grades at school or being praised by his elders. Maybe it was because he could actually see his progress, or maybe it was because he knew *why* he was working, but Karl Kreutz thought washing windows must be the most satisfying of occupations. When Mrs. Phillips drove up and walked into the store it occurred to Karl that window washing would never make one rich.

Mrs. Phillips had lots of money. The Phillips family drove the best automobiles and wore the most expensive clothes. What was more unusual, however, was that they didn't own the big house they lived in, and they ate at the hotel several times every week. None of the old families of the town would have considered living in a rented house if they could afford to buy one. And eating at the hotel in their hometown was a luxury to which people like the Kreutzes rarely treated themselves. The Phillipses had been in town for about a year, and nobody knew much about them. Karl's father had called them "new rich," and Karl had gotten the impression that it was not a complimentary term.

Mrs. Phillips was talking to Mr. Levy and pointing to an old marble-topped dresser which stood against the wall. Why would Mrs. Phillips, who could afford the best and latest of everything, want to buy an old second-hand piece of furniture, Karl wondered. Almost all the old families in town had such furnishings in their homes.

Washing the window, Karl thought again about the boys at his school and how different he felt from them. Maybe if he imitated the other boys, pretended to be like them, they would take him into their crowd. They might change their minds about his being a sissy. After a while maybe he would have secured his reputation so well that they would like him even if he went back to being himself. He had just about decided to give the experiment a try when a car drove up behind him and stopped. Karl turned and was surprised to see Martin Kreutz get out of the automobile.

"Look, Papa. I'm washing the window," he called happily to his father, who was now at the door of the shop. It took only a second for Karl to perceive that his father was angry with him. Was it later than he realized? Was it after the time he should have been at Aunt Anna's house to meet his father?

All the man did was to say in a low but rather harsh tone of voice, "Get into the car and wait for me!"

Karl was deeply hurt by his father's speaking so abruptly to him. Papa had never been so sharp with him before. But what upset Karl most of all was seeing the window, partly covered with soap and partly glowing in the light of the sunset. He had not finished his job, and he did not dare disobey by trying to complete the work before his father came out of the store. He had tried very hard to do the work well, but since he had not finished, he was not entitled to the vase, and he would have to find something else, something that cost less and would probably not be as pretty, to give to Miss Rogers.

Through the open door of the store Karl could see his father and Mr. Levy talking. For the most part, Mr. Levy was just listening. The storekeeper nodded and reached under the counter for a package which he handed to Martin, who dug into his pocket and gave the other man, something which, Karl supposed, was a coin.

Papa had paid for the vase. As usual, Papa had settled everything. He would think that since Mr. Levy had his money and Karl had his vase, everything was fine, everyone should be satisfied. Papa wouldn't understand that he had wanted more than anything to be allowed to finish his job and feel he had earned the vase. Papa would not understand.

Martin Kreutz returned to the automobile and started the engine as soon as he got in.

"Here's your vase," he said to Karl as he gave him the package. There was restrained irritation in his voice which was not entirely hidden from his son, who quietly held the little parcel in his hands.

"Why didn't you simply ask me for the money, if you wanted the vase so much?" Martin asked. "I'm not unreasonable about giving you what you want."

"No, sir," Karl answered simply, his face very quiet and serious.

"I do not want my son to degrade himself by doing such common work, especially on the public sidewalk," Martin said emphatically. "What will people think?"

Billy Westbrook could have a paper route, because his father was a plumber; and Lucille Meyer could be a babysitter on Saturdays and Sundays, because her father was a grocery clerk. But Karl Kreutz was the son of a wealthy ranchman, and what would people think?

Miss Rogers would have her vase, and he would continue to be called teacher's pet and a sissy.

"I don't care," Karl muttered, his lips twitching with emotion. "I don't care." And it was then that he first knew the agony of being too miserable to cry.

Kindermaskenball
1939

*I*t was a fine day, the sort of blue-sky, warm-sun weather you can feel even before you open your eyes to verify the impression. With only her white muslin nightgown between her and the soft current of spring air which drifted in through the open window by the foot of her bed, Annalies lay there enjoying the delights of mere somatic existence. Prolonged awakening was an extravagance in which she could rarely indulge, but this was Saturday, more particularly, the Saturday of the Children's Masquerade.

Annalies could hear the radio downstairs though it was tuned to a volume which would enable her mother to recognize the too-cheerful voice of the news announcer, without forcing her to listen to the program now in progress, a group of pseudo-cowboys inartistically rendering western ballads. The radio, their first, had been a Christmas gift of Annalies' parents to each other. The way they took all the make-believe and surprises out of Christmas, it was no wonder grown-ups didn't have much fun, she thought. Christmas Eve they had all sat around the tree listening to Madame Schumann-Heink sing *"Stille Nacht, Heilige Nacht"*—from New York, Papa had said. For once Annalies had felt justified in doubting her father's word; it seemed too incredible. Grossvater sat in the big mahogany chair, and Annalies noticed him take out a crumpled handkerchief, blow his nose rather loudly, and brush his moustache with his thumb and forefinger, as he often did when he was thinking unshared thoughts.

Only a week before Grossmutter's death, Annalies had gone with her father to visit his parents. She had taken with her as a gift a pincushion her mother had made from a little square of cloth which the girl had embroidered. In return Grossmutter had given her a small gingham handkerchief she had just finished hemming by hand and a sheet from the latest *Holland's Magazine,* on which was printed a paper-doll with several dresses for it.

Visits with her father's parents were always pleasant events. The four of them would gather in the little sunparlor at the back of the house, and the two men would talk, while Grossmutter rolled cigarettes with a little machine which came as a premium with half a dozen packages of a certain popular brand of tobacco. The old man, whose health seemed to be none the worse for the lifelong habit, smoked continually, using as a cigarette holder a little bamboo tube which looked as if he might have whittled it himself. On the table was a bowl of anise cookies on which the reliefs of birds, flowers, and fruits had been printed with a carved rolling pin brought from the old country. Of these Annalies would consume her capacity while she looked at magazines which had arrived since her last visit. One for farmers and ranchers particularly appealed to her because of the page of letters from the subscribers' children, telling what they did in school, how they had taught their pets tricks, and other similarly weighty communications. Annalies had always wanted to write the woman who edited the column, but since she had never had a pet and could scarcely write that she did not like the school she attended, she postponed the project until such time as she would have something interesting to say. *The Hausfrau* was, for the most part, rather dull reading, but occasionally short poems were used to fill the space at the bottom of the page, and these Annalies read with great interest, feeling, when she especially liked one, that it was certainly destined to be a classic. Sometimes she would read one of them to her grandmother, who usually commented only with a particular brand of smile peculiar to the old, half of amusement and half of indulgence. Once, with the deepest pathos of which her small voice was capable, she had read a long poem to her grandmother, who continued all the while to sew. When Annalies had come to the last two lines:

> Ich habe genossen das irdische Glück:
> Ich habe gelebt und geliebet.

> *I have enjoyed earthly happiness:*
> *I have lived and loved.*

Her grandmother had no longer been able to restrain herself; and when she had added, "Don't you think this Friedrich Schiller should someday be famous?" her grandmother had actually laughed. After such an unsympathetic response, Annalies had been more cautious about sharing these gems of verse.

After Papa and Grossvater had thoroughly summarized the condition of the crops, the market price of cattle, and the latest innovations in farm implements, the conversation would usually turn to the subject of politics. Over steaming coffee the three adults talked of things Annalies could not understand and which she found extremely dull. Shut out of their world, she would retreat into her own.

In the dining room there was a small glass cupboard in which Grossmutter kept all the useless little things which constituted a kind of adjunct to the family Bible. There was an ashtray shaped like a lily pad over which a crane bent its long neck, poised to seize an over-sized frog. A paperweight in the form of two little pigs playing the violin and flute stood on another shelf. Next to it were three small china mugs on which were painted landscapes. Grossmutter had once told her which one Annalies' father had used when he was a little boy. Attempts to imagine her father and his two brothers as children were futile. On the top shelf lay a number of small recuerdos which Grossvater's mother had brought from cities she had visited. One was a little silver snuff-box on the top of which was a circle of china which pictured Schlosz Godesberg. Ahne—*Ancestress*, as the family had called the old lady—had bought it on her last trip to the Rhineland, where she had spent her girlhood.

From what she knew of it, Annalies considered Ahne's life to have been a supremely interesting one, though replete with the sadness of early widowhood during a period when the aftermath of the War Between the States had made supporting a large family in a country not yet quite her home a doubly difficult necessity. In her old age, after her sons had established themselves and her daughters had acquired substantial husbands, she had quit teaching school to avail herself of her independence by traveling widely and writing of her experiences. To Annalies the little snuff-box was like a fragment of a meteorite, part of another world which she remembered but had never seen, and which she idealized as an exile in his native land.

The visit had been much like the others, but Grossmutter had died the next week. Annalies had found everything very hard to understand. She had never before been permitted to go to a funeral, and this was the first death in her family since before her birth. The stout old lady lying there in the large gray coffin had seemed almost like a stranger. There were two little oval impressions on either side of the delicate bridge of the fine, straight nose where spectacles were accustomed to rest, and the still hands, darkly spotted with age, had never seemed so quiet. Annalies remembered when Grossmutter had once pinched a bit on skin on the back of her hand and how it had stood there like a little wave, then slowly receded. Annalies had tried the trick on her own fat little hand over and over again, till Grossmutter had laughed and said, "Altklug magst du sein, aber alt, Gott sei 'dank', noch lange nicht!—*You may be precocious, but old, thank God, not yet!*" Grossmutter and she had laughed so many times together.

The nuns had said that those who were not good Catholics would not go to Heaven. Grossmutter had been baptized a Catholic, but Annalies had never known her to go to church. Perhaps that was why Grossvater always seemed so sad now. The nuns said many things which were frightening. Her parents had sent her to the Catholic school because the public school would not accept her when, at five, she had insisted on starting. Somehow, year after year, she had continued to go to the Catholic school instead of going to the public school with her cousin, Karl.

Annalies' reflections were suddenly interrupted by her

father's footfalls on the sidewalk as he returned from the post office. Papa insisted on punctuality, and he would not permit anyone to come to the table unless properly dressed.

The open door of her clothes closet caught her attention. She hoped that just this once Mama would not have noticed, because a scolding would mar the perfection of the day. As she reached inside for the dark skirt and white middy blouse which hung neatly together on one coat hanger, her eyes fell upon her costume. Mama must have stayed up half the night finishing it, and in her drowsiness forgotten to shut the closet door. It was funny how often parents forgot to abide by the rules they so strictly enforced.

The brightly colored sequins glittered in the semidarkness of the closet like as many stars against a sky of dark red flannel. In the middle of the front of the skirt was a constellation in the shape of a bronze-colored eagle with a shiny green snake in its golden bill. His claws rested on a green prickly-pear bush. The white blouse had little puffed sleeves and a low-cut oval neckline around which were red, white, and green beads in a design of leaves and flowers. Annalies' sisters, Elsbeth and Johanne, had brought the costume from Mexico City with them the summer before, but their mother had gathered the waistline tighter and shortened the skirt so that Annalies would be able to wear it. The blouse she would wear was not the one which had come with the skirt, but one which Mama had copied from the original so accurately that only size distinguished them.

Annalies reluctantly closed the closet door, slipped the dark skirt and the middy over her little coronet of ash-blond braids, and smoothed them over her loose-fitting white slip. Growing children, Mama said, should have their clothes hanging from the shoulders, because tight waistbands were not healthful for the very young. But this afternoon she would wear the costume, which not only had a tight waistband, but a wide sash which went around the waist, crossed in back, and came over the shoulders to be tucked under the girdle it formed in front.

This would probably be the last *Kindermaskenball* in which she would take part, because next year she would go to public high school, and the boys and girls there felt they were too old for such activities. Just now Annalies was uncertain whether growing up was worth the price.

Since the soft soles of her tennis shoes would muffle the sound, she felt safe in bounding down the steps two at a time, then walked into the breakfast room with the dignity befitting a young lady.

When Papa had left for the quarry and the older girls were clearing the table, Annalies carried the kitchen stool to the back porch, so that she could sit high enough for Mama to braid her hair without stooping.

"Mrs. Wendlein called and said Luise would not be able to be your partner in the parade. Father Weber said that since she was going to enter the convent when school is out, it would not be proper for her to take part in a masquerade and dance." Mama spoke in her usual soft voice, but Annalies could sense her irritation. The *Kindermaskenball* was an event whose name alone brought back memories which the sands of time had burnished beyond their original brilliance. With almost fearful consciousness of the impermanence of youth, the woman spent much of her time staging happy little experiences with which her children would be able to fortify themselves during the sadder years she knew would come. Her only moments of bad humor came when something or someone interfered with her carefully laid plans for such occasions, and the family, misinterpreting her irritability for fatigue, tried to discourage her elaborate preparations.

Months before, the children had begun to choose their

partners for the masquerade. During the early years the festivities had been held during Lent, which the local Protestants did not observe very strictly. Though the event now always took place late in the spring, Catholic parents, for whom the *Kindermaskenball* did not hold such rich associations, did not have the same enthusiasm for the tradition which the Protestants guarded and preserved so fondly for their children.

"She said Luise is very sorry and hopes you will find someone else to march with you," Annalies heard her mother continue.

"I don't know anyone else to ask," Annalies said, after a silence in which she had mentally scanned the school register.

"I will phone Tante Frieda and ask her to have Karl march with you," Annalies' mother decided. "Don't worry, we'll arrange it all so you'll have a good time. There now, run along and help the girls with the dishes," she said, as she left the distressed little girl alone to contemplate the unwelcome turn of events.

It was better, she supposed, to march with your cousin than to have one of the teachers who supervised the masquerade pair you off with another child who was alone. But she knew Karl would not be happy about being forced to escort his young cousin who did not fit in with his public school friends. She knew it was not that Karl did not like her, because when they were alone together he seemed to enjoy talking as much as she did, and once when they had been playing house in the woodshed he had given her a little ring which he had made out of a horseshoe nail. The worst part of all was that he was going to masquerade as a sailor, and the incongruity of their costumes would betray that their marching together was a last-minute decision.

The morning passed quickly with everyone in the house keyed to holiday pitch. Lunch was late because the picnic spread had to be prepared. When Mama planned a picnic, the meal and the equipment were so complete that one never encountered the need of borrowing from the neighboring tables. She had even provided for several extra people in the event that there should be unexpected guests.

Almost before anyone realized it, the time had come to dress for the parade. Annalies felt like a queen with the three ladies in waiting volunteering their help in all details of her toilette. Finally she ventured a look at herself in the long mirror on Mama's closet door. Only fear of ruining the unfamiliar rouge which Elsbeth had applied on her cheeks kept her from crying for joy. The long gathered skirt concealed the flat hips and the knees, usually red with Mercurochrome, which would have stamped her as the tom-boy she was. The fullness of the dainty white blouse and snugly fitting girdle almost completed the illusion of some feminine contours. Above it all was the round little face on which was a matched pair of dimples which, her brother, Franz, had once told her, were little pageboys who turned on the lights in her eyes and drew back her lips so her pretty teeth could take a curtain call. The masquerade came so soon after the Easter holidays that he would be able to see her in her splendid costume only through the medium of the snapshots which would be sent to him at college. Mama and the girls took turns posing her with the best portions of the garden for background. The end of a roll of film and the increasing numbers of children who drifted past the house signaled the approach of the hour at which the parade was to assemble at the high school.

Each grade had been assigned a room in which to meet, and in each members of the teaching staff were trying to organize their excited charges. While the other children pranced around nervously, unable to hide their impatience, Annalies sat quietly and apart, surveying the walls of the unfamiliar classroom. On one green plaster wall was a picture of an Indian on a horse riding into the sunset. Several feet away was a picture of Wilhelm Tell with his arm about his son. Over the teacher's desk was a large photograph of an old man with a very long beard. Annalies recognized the name under the picture as that of the man who, Mama had said, had planned the original *Kindermaskenball.*

Long ago, when Grossmutter had been a little girl, the town's schoolmaster had inaugurated the custom to raise money for enlarging the library of the academy. For many years since, state agencies had fulfilled the function of the old man's highly successful plan. The affair was now merely a costume ball rather than a masquerade, but it still retained its original name, most of its features, and all of its popularity. Even grown-ups responded to the excitement of the day, as all the activity in and around the school building clearly bore witness.

Finally Miss Henschel managed to get the sixth-graders arranged in double file and marched them down to the school grounds to their place behind the younger children.

Annalies was so thankful that Karl did not seem much upset by having his plans disrupted that she did not even question him to find out how he had disposed of his original partner. The public school children were chattering excitedly amongst themselves as the American Legion Band struck up a marching tune, and, as if singing a madrigal in which the parts bore no relation to one another, the bands from the various schools added their simpler melodies. First came the tiny pre-school children, some in perambulators, herded along by those of their parents who felt most able to undergo the strain. Most of these young men and women were the boys and girls who had only a decade before been in the rear ranks of the procession. Now and then someone would shout a greeting from the curb to one or another of the young mothers who had moved to a neighboring town as a bride. The behavior of the children was as entertaining to the bystanders as were the costumes. Tiny ballerinas in pink tarlatan and acrobats too young to walk were interspersed with cowboys and war-painted Indians who clung to their mothers' skirts.

After the Legionnaires came the primary school children, terribly self-assured and conscious of the onlookers. Past Gerlich's Garage they came, followed by the Carl Schurz School Band, with their maroon capes lined with gold-colored satin and jauntily flung over their shoulders. Around the depot was the usual group of old men who gathered there to smoke and chat. The people in Henne's Hardware Store and Dr. Halm's second-story office waved and called to the children in the street below. The Opera House was not showing a movie that afternoon. Hastily, Karl dashed out of the parade to buy a bag of wine-drops in Kaufmann's Candy Kitchen and ran back to his place beside Annalies in the slow-moving line.

Behind the Lamar School Band came the older children. Many of the costumes which had been worn in Miss Bachmann's Dancing School recitals made a second appearance here on the same or different models. A few had been made in another country or another generation. Almost every year there were a few predominant motifs. Last year there had been fully a dozen Indians and as many cowboys. This year the Oriental influence seemed to hold precedence, unless one placed all the peasant costumes, authentic and otherwise, in one category. The men in Loep's Butcher Shop with their white aprons rolled around their middles and the clerks from Jacob Schmidt and Sons, Dry Goods, crowded up to the curbs as the strange caravan passed. The high-school crowd came out of Richter's Drug Store to watch their younger brothers and sisters while trying to hide their interest under veils of sophistication. Half-emptied cups of coffee were forgotten in Ed Moeller's Cafe, and men without their hats and coats deserted the chairs in Pete Wagenfuehr's Barber Shop to get a glimpse at the next generation's businessmen and housewives.

"Hey, George, ain't bankers' hours enough, but you have to take time off to loaf on a street corner?" one man in a blue workshirt jovially called to the president of the First National Bank.

"Those are my boys out there," the well-dressed man called back, proudly pointing to a handsome dark boy and a smaller blond one walking in the Boy Scouts' section.

The parade rounded the plaza, getting smaller all the time as the little ones reluctantly dropped out to join their waiting parents. Like most of the other children, Annalies was feeling very hot and tired, but nothing could have persuaded her to admit it.

The blue-and-white-uniformed high school band marched by, still playing loudly rather than well.

As an appendage to the multi-colored line weaving its way down the street came the Lone Oak Band. It was a sundry group of men of all ages with a stout, middle-aged man, a local barkeeper, at its head. The cap of his uniform, if a white shirt and trousers warrant the application of the name, sat precariously on its nest of bushy, gray hair. One moment of listening made clear the title "Ach und Krach Band—*Sigh and Crash Band*" with which a local wit had re-baptized it.

The crowd dispersed behind what was left of the original group of marchers. Being able to walk all the way to the park in the heat of the afternoon signified a certain accomplishment which was the goal of every child. By the time the Comal Creek bridge came into view, the weary little group could scarcely be called a parade. The pavement was hot beneath their feet from long hours of exposure to the April sun. Some of the more adventurous boys broke the ranks to explore the banks of the creek. The danger of rattlesnakes acted only as an additional lure, and those boys whose costumes escaped injury from the dense, semi-tropical vegetation and muddy ground were as rare as they were fortunate. This was one of Annalies' favorite places to play, but she remained on the bridge with the others who were looking on excitedly.

Attention shifted from the fish-like odor which hung in the sultry air around Dittlinger Roller Mills to the huge power plant, resting like a steamer at anchorage in a smooth ocean of green lawn. Once inside Landa Park, the children found a variety of amusements. A few ventured their first swim of the season in the cold Comal River, but the less intrepid chose boating or dancing. In one of the dance pavillions some local instrumentalists played traditional German dance tunes, while in the other a young man of the town conducted a group of his contemporaries in playing new American jazz with a distinctly German twist.

From infancy many of the children had accompanied their parents to the Bürgerbaëlle—*Citizens Balls*, so that dancing was to them no new experience. They knew the schottisch from the waltz and switched from one to the other with enviable facility. Age and sex played little part in the selection of partners, and when a couple tired of the old-fashioned dances, they could walk a hundred yards and sample the modern repertory, so that both groups were continually changing.

After Karl had fulfilled his duty of dancing the first few sets with Annalies and had provided her with a bottle of soda water, he felt free to join his other playmates. Had the afternoon been longer she would certainly have been ill, for in order not to be conspicuously a wallflower, she managed always to be busy with a bottle of pop or some ice-cream.

At six the music stopped and the children went to join their families at pre-arranged places for supper. Annalies found her family laying the table near one big oak which had perversely grown horizontally after the first few feet of trunk and had been propped up with concrete supports. Strands of brightly colored lights and beards of Spanish moss made the huge old oaks and elms look like giant Christmas trees under which story-book characters were holding a convention.

In the course of the meal old acquaintances stopped by to exchange friendly greetings. A lady from a neighboring table came over to borrow a bottle-opener. Annalies' parents had always insisted that whenever possible she answer in the language in which she was addressed, but this presented one great difficulty. Having learned two languages (and a smattering of Spanish for good measure) as a small child, she was not always certain which words belonged to each language.

"Wie geht's dir denn?—*How are you?*" the lady asked.

"All right," she answered.

"Kannst du kein Deutsch sprechen?—*Can't you speak any German?*" the lady asked in surprise.

"'Sure," the child answered, surprised at the adults' amusement. Grown-ups seemed always either to be ridiculing or scolding children, but she was accustomed to older people and had long ago ceased trying to understand them.

Supper over, all the family returned to the dance hall. Only the jazz orchestra played in the evening, and the high-school crowd waited restlessly for the hour when the little children would have to clear the floor for them. Parents lined the walls of the hall so that they might be available to satisfy the demand for additional nickels and act as repositories for jackets and pocketbooks.

Annalies sat sadly between her parents wishing she were in ordinary clothes so she would not be so conspicuous. Even the nice compliments which Mama's friends paid her seemed to be calculated to console her. The older people talked of their memories of other masquerades and all around her, the children seemed so gay that she felt she must be the first child who had not enjoyed the fete.

Even when Karl finally came over and asked her to dance, she was no happier, because she felt he was merely fulfilling an obligation. After they had danced one set together without talking, Karl began almost apologetically, "Phyllis is here." Phyllis, she knew, was the partner he had originally asked. "She has a cold, but her mother let her come for the grand march."

It was just as well, she thought. She was resigned to watching the others.

"I have a partner for you," Karl continued, anxious to make amends. "He just moved to town and doesn't know hardly anybody. His daddy is going to open a dry-goods store here."

She was glad the other boy didn't know many of the children. Maybe people would think he had really asked her to be his partner. Her eagerness was even harder to restrain when Karl steered her toward a boy in a Mexican charro costume, the perfect complement to her China Poblana.

He was a strange little boy, smaller than she and younger looking, but almost all the boys in her class were smaller than the girls. There was something almost comical about the sad, deep-set eyes shaded by the wide brim of the black sombrero and the round body enveloped by the close-fitting breeches. Karl had said he was Jewish; Annalies wondered what it was about a person that made him a Jew. She was glad that he didn't talk much, because she would not have known what to say.

"How old are you?" David finally asked after Karl had left them alone.

"Twelve."

"I'm thirteen," he asserted proudly. "What school do you go to?"

"I go to the Catholic school, but I'm going to the high school next year," she said, trying to sound pleased.

"Me too," he said. "What does your father do?"

"He manages a rock quarry."

"My dad's going to open a dry-goods store. He's in New York buying some of the merchandise now."

"I was in New York once," she said, wishing she could remember what it had been like so that she would have something to talk about. She was rescued from the impasse in the conversation by an amplified voice from the orchestra shell, announcing the grand march.

They took their places in the line, and the march was underway. First they marched double-file around the hall, then came down the middle. Then alternating couples went in opposite directions and they marched four abreast. The division was continued until there were eight people in every row and then the unravelling began. Finally the head couple faced each other and clasped hands to form an arch for the others. Soon the couples had formed a tunnel through which the others had to pass. When everyone had passed through, the couples marched around the hall once more as in the beginning, and at the signal all rushed to the center in a noisy finale.

The celebration was over, and the children cleared the floor for the grown-ups. Mothers collected their spent little broods and settled them in their coats to protect them against the cool night air.

Annalies' mother was saying, "I can't understand why the young people like that loud jazz music. When I was a girl . . . ." Her voice lost itself in the noise made by the dozens of automobile motors as they hummed into action.

Annalies climbed into the back seat of their sedan and took off her slippers.

"Mama," she called in a happy, drowsy voice.

"Ja," her mother answered wearily.

"David asked me to go to the first high-school dance with him next fall," she said dreamily.

Papa glanced in the rear-view mirror at the sleeping little figure.

"Na, Alte—*Well, Old Girl*," he affectionately grasped his wife's hand in the darkness, "looks like we have another Bakfisch—*girl on the brink of womanhood*—on our hands."

The Man With Big Ideas
1940

*I*t is the business of the Secretary of the Chamber of Commerce to know and exploit whatever distinctions a town has, and Jesse Kincaid was full of ideas. Of the natural beauties and other assets which had caused the Mainzer Adelsverein to choose this site for its settlement in 1844 he was thoroughly cognizant. And that the town had not maintained its rank as the fourth largest city in Texas (according to the 1850 census) was the source of his most constant annoyance.

"What this town needs," he told Mayor Walter Freitag, "is something to give it national publicity. When you read a paper you don't read the ads. What *do* you read first when you get the morning paper?"

"Well, first I take a quick glance at the headlines," the mayor answered, then added, "Say, you aren't suggesting we stage something sensational just to make the front page, are you?"

"Of course not," Jesse Kincaid said, filing the idea away for future reference. "What do you read after the headlines?"

"Usually the sports section, I guess," Walter said. He was a football enthusiast.

"That's it! You've got it!" Kincaid shouted as he whirled around in his swivel chair. In one carefully worded letter he had convinced the manager of the Philadelphia Phillies that New Braunfels, Texas, was the ideal place for a baseball team to train for its season.

One afternoon a few weeks later Jesse and Walter were parked at the Missouri Pacific Depot awaiting the arrival of the ball club from the North. Jesse Kincaid was nervous. This was his first big project since he had taken the job in the city hall of the little community, and he knew that whether he stayed or not depended largely on the success of this undertaking. Up to now it had been almost impossible for him to get the cooperation of the local people who, though friendly, seemed to feel that the town would continue to thrive without systematized publicity. He liked the little burg, but he found its leisurely pace and apparently unambitious conservatism profoundly irritating to his energetic Yankee mind. No one ever seemed in much of a hurry to get anywhere or to do anything. For example, the railroad station before him was a veritable symbol of the character of the town. This yellow-painted frame building formed the background for a group of old men whose least common denominator was long hours of idleness.

"You know," Jesse said as he turned to his companion, "it's a disgrace the way those old fellows over there give the impression that this town hasn't got enough work to keep everyone busy. After one look at them a newcomer would decide that the town was half dead and didn't give a damn. I've a good mind to talk to the authorities about putting up a sign in the depot to keep people like that from hanging around."

"I wouldn't do that if I were you," Walter answered. "People wouldn't appreciate it much. No sirree."

Walter Freitag knew what he was talking about. Having spent all the fifty years of his life in the little town, he knew how stubborn the people could be when someone tried to change something to which they were attached. Looking at the men, he realized how familiar they were although with some of them he had never had occasion to exchange more than a greeting.

The nucleus of the group was the friendly, stout little man whose sole job was to halt the San Antonio Street traffic a few times daily when trains approached. Very few people remembered that old Joachim Kreutz was the son of a German nobleman who had fled to Texas during the mid-nineteenth century revolutions. Three of Joachim's older brothers had joined the Confederate Army, but only one had returned. Like so many of the first generation born in the new country, Joachim had never really been to school. With the help of books brought from Europe, his father had given the children lessons after each day's work on the farm. English they had learned from Mr. Lyons, a private tutor who had also taught Walter's father when he was a boy.

For years a general store in an outlying community had been the source of Joachim's income, but the boll weevil had forced him to sell out at a great loss. Now, though he was past eighty, Joachim was still an active member of the local Schützenverein—*Defense Society*—and every fall would go deer hunting in the cedar hills where he had spent his boyhood.

When King George V of England died, many commented on the resemblance of the newspaper photographs to old Joachim Kreutz with his short gray beard and dignified bearing. Joachim only chuckled when he heard that and went on telling his hunter's tales in the slow, south-German dialect of his aristocratic ancestors.

Sometimes when he got lonesome for the railroad, old Werner Homann would leave the little sun-baked brick cabin he shared with his bachelor brother and walk down to the station to watch the afternoon southbound come in. Winter or summer, he wore a black sateen shirt and the stiff, black felt hat with its round, high crown and narrow brim which was the most conspicuous difference between him and his brother Max, whose hat was wider and had creases in the top.

It took Werner nearly ten minutes to walk the two blocks to the depot because of the leg injury which had terminated his days as a brakeman and provided him with a pension. At the station he would refill his antique corn-cob pipe and sit down in a chair beside the other old men who had gathered there. Sometimes they would talk; again they would smoke in silence while the burnt matches fell in a small semi-circle at their feet.

When the conductor had shouted "all aboard," Werner limped down the street to Ma's Cafe to have his daily glass of beer, then continued on his way toward home. Usually he would pass Miss Mina Kreutz's house, where old Sam Guffy had a room. Walter's mother, who often visited Miss Kreutz, had been greatly amused when she told her son how, if Werner was in one of his rare garrulous moods, he would run his cane along the pickets of the fence as a signal for Sam to come out for a chat.

Sam Guffy was one of the city's veteran night-watchmen. If there was anything he liked better than talking about the time he had captured the men who had tried to rob the First National Bank, it was telling of his boyhood experiences as one of the original Chisholm Trail drivers. Each year the Texas Trail Drivers would have a ball in San Antonio, and Sam would come back with his old stories revitalized and embellished with new details. Walter had heard these stories many times since he had begun to occupy the mayor's office.

Sam had been a widower for years, but his room and his clothing had the appearance of being cared for by a meticulous woman. Whenever Sam went out, his shoes were a shiny ebony, his black suit was pressed, and his white shirt was spotlessly fresh. To every woman who passed he tipped his black ten-gallon hat with an exaggerated chivalry which made young girls giggle and their mothers beam with admiration.

There was never anything gallant in the manner of Hans Meissner. During twenty-five years as janitor of the public high school, he had become so familiar with the personalities, pranks, and puppy-love affairs of most of the residents under forty years of age that false dignity was short-lived in his presence. Since they were both city employees, Hans always greeted Walter as if he were a partner in a business of great importance.

Hans was a nephew of the first German settler who crossed the Guadalupe River when their caravan moved up from Indianola on the coast to Las Fontanas, where they had built their town. Hans' cousin was a city commissioner. Another cousin had been postmaster. In short, Hans Meissner thought himself as securely pedigreed as if his ancestors had come over on the *Mayflower* in 1620 instead of on the *Johann Dethart* in 1844.

Now and then, when the school was closed on a holiday, Hans would go down to the station just to sit and talk to the ticket agent or whoever might be about. During the Depression one of the high school boys had confided in Hans his plan to hop a freight and find work elsewhere. Half that night the man stayed around the station, but the boy outwitted him and waited to board the train after it left the city limits. Somehow Hans felt he had failed in his duty to the parents of the town when the boy disappeared for several years.

Trains have carried many a small-town boy away from home to deceptively greener fields. Eddie Reinhard knew railroad stations all over the country. He probably was more at home in a train than in a house. When he was a boy, Eddie got the notion that blowing his trombone might pay off better than the few bottles of beer each member of the little dance band got for playing at a Bürgerball.

One day Eddie stopped hoeing cotton long enough to watch a circus train pass on its way to San Antonio. He managed to borrow the money to go to one performance, but he rode his bicycle the thirty miles to save railroad fare. The band was wonderful and the uniforms spectacular. Even if they wouldn't take him as a musician, Eddie figured he might go along as a stable boy. He knew about horses, being a farmer's son. But the bandmaster liked him and his trombone, and Eddie joined the circus.

When he inherited his father's farm, Eddie sold the land to Walter's uncle so he would not have any ties. Every fall he came back home with his pockets full of cash, but each spring he had to go back to earn enough money to keep himself alive the next winter. As he grew old, he longed to settle down, but after a few days at home he would grow restless to move on. Then he would leave his room and go to the depot to watch the trains come in, or wander about the streets in the hope of finding some crony with whom he could share boyhood memories over a game of skat at Streuer's Saloon.

Eddie Reinhard rarely thought of himself as a failure. He was not in the least inclined toward introspection. In fact, when he would meet Ernst Weisz at the railroad station, he felt a sort of condescending pity for the other man.

Mediocre talents always have in them an element of tragedy. Sometimes showmanship augments competence and passes for genius. But Ernst Weisz was neither an exhibitionist nor a virtuoso. He was seventeen before he decided that he wanted to be a concert violinist, and then his teachers declared him too old to ever develop his technique fully. Too old at seventeen! Discouraged, he returned from New York and began to teach music to the children of the little town. Walter Freitag had been one of those children.

Ernst had been concertmaster of a group of instrumentalists which ambitiously called itself a symphony orchestra. When the old man who was its conductor died, Ernst took his place. Adequate patronage had always been the least worry of any musical effort in the community. Since its beginning the town had had more than its share of eager amateur performers. But in the late 30's all the younger men joined the National Guard, for martial music and uniforms had a wide appeal with which the sedate classics could not compete.

Someone in the city hall got the idea that the town

should capitalize on its beauties as a resort by organizing a summer camp for young musicians. Well-known professors and conductors were assembled, and youngsters from Texas high schools came to study and to play in the much advertised Landa Park. On registration day, the faculty members, strangers in the town, were somewhat surprised to see a tall, gaunt old man with a violin case stand in line to pay his fees.

Having grown deaf, Ernst Weisz could not hear the instructions which the conductor gave, and sometimes, when concentrating on the score, the old man would not notice the conductor sweep his baton downward to signal for silence. Then the youthful musicians would turn and listen with reverent attention to the perfectly executed violin solo which drifted with delicate sadness on the summer breeze.

Though he could not share in most of their conversation, Ernst often joined the group who gathered at the depot. Somehow just being there among men of his own age made him feel a bit less isolated from the world. When the train whistled in the distance he turned with them to look down the track.

Walter and Jesse heard the whistle and got out of the automobile in which they had been sitting. Each of the old men greeted Walter by his given name as he and his companion passed the depot. Jesse received only an appraising glance and a collective "Good afternoon" from the group in response to the tipping of his hat.

"Wer ist der fremde Kerl—*Who is the strange fellow?*" Werner Homann asked.

"That's the new secretary of the chamber of commerce," answered Sam Guffy, who could understand German but could not speak it.

"Ich hab' gehört der hät' grosze Rosinen im Sack—*I've heard that he has big raisins in the sack, or big ideas,*" Joachim Kreutz added dryly and walked away to stop the traffic for the train to pass. The others chuckled.

"What did he say?" Ernst Weisz asked, cupping his hand behind one ear.

"He said the young fellow has plans for changing our town to a big city," Sam Guffy repeated in a loud voice.

Someday, Vielleicht
1940

Some days were just not meant to run smoothly, and that this was one of them Emma Hoffmann would certainly have agreed. Heinrich had already been waiting with the car by the side of the house when the trouble started. As she hurriedly reached up to shut the draft of the kitchen stove, some of its shiny blackness had come off onto the front of her skirt. Even the necessity for changing dresses would have been distressing enough, but she was determined to wear this particular dress, and today, because by the next time she would go to town to market, the weather would be too cool for cotton.

All the while Emma was carrying the water indoors and

laying extra wood on the fire to heat the iron, she dreaded Heinrich's irritation at the delay. Town women, with their electrical appliances and modern equipment, could never conceive of the difficulty of managing a household without even the convenience of running water.

As she stood there in her cotton slip and her black straw sailor hat rubbing the black smudge out of the white and blue cloth, she held up the simple dress for an admiring look. It had taken several weeks to match four of the brightly printed sacks in which the locally milled Dittlinger's Flour was packaged. Using buttons from an old discarded dress and the same pattern by which almost all her dresses had been cut, with slight alterations in the trim-ming, she had been able to make a nice dress for less than a dollar, a small fraction of the price she would have had to pay for the cheapest ready-made equivalent. Heinrich never seemed to realize how much money she saved him by her cleverness, but she got a tremendous amount of satis-faction out of her frugality.

She could hear him, outside, whistling tunelessly as he always did when he was growing impatient. Finally, when the iron was hot enough, she pressed out the damp spot, hastily slipped into the dress, and was still fumbling with the buttons, which extended from the neckline to the hem, as she closed the door of the house. Before she had com-pletely shut the door of the Model-A, Heinrich had already started the car into motion. Emma smoothed the large bun of hair at the back of her neck, moistened her finger to rub the too-pink powder out of her eyebrows, and took one more look at her large, middle-aged face in the little pocket mirror.

Silently she got out to open the gate when Heinrich brought the car to an abrupt halt. For once she was glad she didn't have white shoes, because the muddy lane would have spoiled them anyway. Even the coarsely gravelled county road seemed smooth by contrast. The road was in the dense green shadow of the cliffs, but on the quiet river the morning sun shone unobscured.

"Die God'lup scheint ho' zu sein—*The Guadalupe seems to be high,*" was the comment with which Heinrich finally broke the silence, as they crossed the Guadalupe River. "It musta rained more than I thought."

"Die Mrs. Welsh hat gesagt sie hät' vier Zoll in 'ne tin can gemessen—*Mrs. Welsh said that she had measured four inches in a tin can,*" Emma added hopefully, but Heinrich let the conversation die unassisted. Nervously she snapped and unsnapped the clasp of her handbag.

By the side of the road a group of Boy Scouts were straightening up the refuse of their camp breakfast. "Ich bin sure froh dasz der Leroy die opportunity gehabt hat die Boy Scouts zu joinen—*I'm sure glad that Leroy has had the opportunity to join the Boy Scouts,*" Emma said. "Ich glaub' das is' recht educational—*I believe that's right educational.*"

"Educational mag's ja sein, aber ich kennt' ihn sure brauchen beim cultivatin'. Dies in die high school geh'n is' sure 'ne expense. I have my doubts ob das ihn je hilft ein besserer farmer zu sein," Heinrich responded. "*Educational it may be, but I know I sure need him in cultivatin' time. This going to high school is sure an expense. I have my doubts if that ever helps him be a better farmer.*"

Emma felt it best not to pursue that topic any further, remembering how much of an argument Heinrich had raised when she had insisted that their son be allowed to continue in town when he had completed the nine grades of the country school.

Heinrich steered the car into the little filling station by the side of the road. "Ein quart lubricatin' ale, the billigest kind you got—*A quarter of lubricatin' oil, the cheapest kind you got,*" he directed the attendant. "Kenn'st auch mein windshield abreiben—*Can you also rub off my windshield?*"

The car started again as if clearing its throat and headed down the paved highway. The big wastepile of Landa's quarry loomed ahead like a pyramid of sand against the dark green of the cedar brush. In passing Emma waved back to the two small Mexican children who played along the railroad track by the side of a little gray shack. In her childhood she had always been disappointed when the enthusiastic greetings she called to the occupants of passing buggies received no response.

Finally the town came into view, first a fringe of small houses and then the outlines of the electrical power plant, the wheat elevator, the county courthouse, and the steeples of the two large churches. Traffic became heavier as they drove through Comal Town, across the bridge over the Comal River, and into the center of town. Heinrich came into town at least once a week, but to Emma a visit to town had never ceased to be exciting. On clear Saturdays such as this, little groups of country people, glad of the opportunity to chat with their friends, would almost block the sidewalk at intervals of a few dozen feet. There were cars parked on both sides of Mill Street from Doeppenschmidt's Funeral Home to the Post Office.

"I wonder who died," Heinrich said.

"In die Post Office gibt's vielleicht eine death notice—*There's perhaps a death notice in the Post Office,*" Emma suggested.

Heinrich went in and brought out the little black-edged piece of paper. "Herbert Jones, aged sixty-two," Gottlieb read. "Das der Amerikaner der die Muellers ranch damals gekauft hat. Der hat viel Geld in oil property gemacht und hat hier sein home gebaut wie er retir'n wollt. Das is' sure some show-place."

"That's the American that bought the Muellers' ranch then. That one made plenty of money in oil property and built his home here for when he wanted to retire. That's sure some show-place."

Not bothering to go to the corner, Heinrich crossed the street in the middle of the block, carrying a plowshare in each hand. While finishing the job in progress, the black-smith, a friendly man, called out a greeting over the ring of the anvil. Finally he laid down the heavy tool and wiped his glowing face with the large red bandanna he had taken from the hip pocket of his striped overalls. Wilhelm Meyer's costume was so consistently the same season after season that it had become almost a uniform. On his head was a dark cap such as one associates with railroad engineers, and the short-sleeved white knit undershirt revealed the well-developed muscles of his shoulders and arms. Heinrich arranged to have the smith leave the sharpened plowshares just outside the door, where he could get at them even after closing time, and returned to the car.

Emma was rechecking her shopping list, balancing the estimate of her expenditures against what she expected to get for her butter and eggs.

"Der Meyer sagt der weather-man hät' gesagt es hät' hier in Braunfels so hart geregnet dasz ein Paar telephone lines 'runter greissen wär'n," Heinrich communicated. "Es wär'n auch ein Paar schlimme car wrecks gewesen hier drausen bei der highway intersection. Es wär'n Leut' aus Sangantone gewesen. Der einer steckt in der calaboose weil er angeschossen gewesen wär'. Noch einer hät' sein skull gefractured und wär' im sanitorium weil das City Hospital so gecrowded wär'."

"Meyer says the weatherman said it rained so hard in Braunfels that a couple of telephone lines were torn down. Also there was a couple of bad car wrecks here out at the high-

way intersection. They were supposed to be folks from San Antonio. One of them was stuck in the calaboose because he was drunk. Another one had a fractured skull and was put in the sanitorium because the city hospital was so crowded."

Emma listened with interest to the latest news, then took one last survey of her appearance. Heinrich, who had never quite mastered the art of driving in downtown traffic, was concerned by now with parking in the only remaining space in front of the county courthouse.

Getting in the back seat of the car, Emma handed Heinrich the large basket with its nine dozen eggs and carried the five pounds of butter herself as they crossed the plaza to Eiband and Fischer's Department Store.

"Was soll's sein?" the grocery clerk asked after he had determined the value of the Hoffmann's butter and eggs.

"Well, ich mecht' erst diese cans gecrushte pineapples auf ein Paar cans geslicete exchangen. Mein Mann hat letzten weekend hier im store beim sale das shoppen getan, und ich war sure disappointed wie er die gecrushten pineapples gebracht hat, denn ich wollt' up-side-down cake fier Sonntag machen. Mein Mann liked den so gut. Ich muss auch shortening und 'ne grosze can Kaffie haben. Gib mir was du denkst ein guter brand ist. Kannst mir auch ein Paar boxen matches und so'ne jar kendy mit geben. Das kannst du dann alles chargen. Mein credit ist doch noch gut?"

"Well, first I'd like these cans of crushed pineapples exchanged for a couple cans of sliced. My husband last weekend did the shopping here because there was a sale, and I was sure disappointed how he brought me the crushed pineapples, because I wanted to make upside-down cake for Sunday. My husband really likes that. I also must have shortening and a large can of coffee. Give me what you think's a good brand. Can you also give me a couple of boxes of matches and also a jar of candy. Then you can charge it all. My credit is good,

yes?" While the clerk helped Emma make her other selections, Heinrich wandered around talking to other farmers who were in the store.

The activity of the grocery department fascinated Emma. The ring of the cash registers mingled with the sybillant hiss of the little containers as they traveled on trolleys overhead with money and back with change. There was a constant din of the voices of dozens of customers and clerks punctuated by the shrill sound of several telephone bells.

Her grocery list checked, Emma assembled her purchases into the basket which Heinrich carried over his arm.

Heinrich started to back cautiously out of the narrow space, but Emma stopped him with, "Da kommt grad' die hearse—*There comes the hearse straight ahead.* We better wait till they pass."

"Der Doeppenschmidt hat sure feine cars. Ich muss erst sterben vor ich in so'ne feine car fahr'n darf—*Doeppenschmidt's sure has fine cars. I'll have to die before I can ride in such a fine car,*" Heinrich commented good-humoredly and Emma smiled at what she knew was supposed to be a joke. "I'll bet der hat die besten taxi-cabs und ambulances in der ganzen Welt—*I'll bet they have the best taxi-cabs and ambulances in the whole world.*"

The funeral procession was short because the dead man was a newcomer in town. The people who had been staring curiously from the sidewalks went on about their activities as the Hoffmanns' car turned down Mill Street. Finally it drew up to the curb in front of a little yellow frame cottage, distinguished from those on either side of it only by the bright red potted geranium on the banister of the small porch. Emma opened the screen door, and they walked in.

The odor of food cooking drifted into the living room and a young, treble voice called, "I'm back here."

Mother and daughter embraced, while Heinrich greeted the young woman in the checked apron.

"Wie geht's hier—*How are things here?*" Emma asked.

"Ach, all right," the young housewife answered without allowing her preparations for lunch to be interrupted. "Der Leroy hilft heut' Morgen den Boy Scouts fier den 'Bundles for Britain' drive zu cullecten. Der kommt aber gleich naher zurick. Und der Charlie is' hinten in die yard die picket-fence am fixen."—*"Leroy is helping the Boy Scouts this morning collecting for the 'Bundles for Britain' drive. But he'll be coming back right away. And Charlie is outside in the yard fixing the picket fence."*

She called out of the window to her husband, "Honey, Mama and Daddy are here."

Heinrich began to mill around restlessly in the tiny kitchen, finally escaping to the slightly larger living room where he settled down with the latest issue of the *Herald*.

Emma was setting the steaming dishes of food on the neatly laid table in one corner of the kitchen when her son-in-law, a tall young Irishman in an army mechanic's fatigue suit, made his noisy entrance onto the scene. There was a cordial exchange of greetings before Leroy's return caused another interruption.

"Habt ihr irgend luck gehabt mit euer'n drive—*Did you have any luck with your drive?*" Emma asked her son.

"Oh, it went O. K., I guess," the boy answered, and Emma immediately sensed that he preferred to speak English. Ever since the children had left home, they had showed a certain reluctance to speak German, and this had become something of a barrier between them and their parents, who did not realize that they themselves could not speak either language without the aid of the other one.

"Ruby Jean tells me you all have been pickin' cotton the last couple o' weeks," Charlie addressed his father-in-law.

"Ja. The county agent said we had a lot less root rot than anybody else around Sattler," the farmer proudly answered in a heavy German accent.

"How do you like my new dress, Ruby Jean?" Emma asked her daughter.

"It's nice, Mama, but I think it should be a little shorter. Mrs. Johnson always says there's nothing that ruins the style of your clothes so much as wearing your dresses too long."

Emma tried to hide her hurt feelings, but she had to admit to herself that her children sometimes seemed a little ashamed of her. Everything about her made it obvious that she was just an ordinary German farmer's wife, and the children seemed to want to be allowed to forget it.

Dinner over, the men retired to the living room, and Emma prepared to help Ruby Jean do the dishes. The noisy slam of the back door announced Leroy's exit, and Emma tried again to re-establish the lost intimacy with her daughter.

"Behaved der Leroy sich all right? Hoff' der gibt euch kein trüble—*Has Leroy behaved all right? Hope he doesn't give you any trouble.*"

"Oh no. Der studied und macht gute grades. Und er hilft mir auch beim house-cleanen. Ich hab' heut Morgen der Mrs. Johnson ihr'n vacuum-cleaner geborgt und hab' die rugs gecleaned. Dann hab' ich das ganze Haus gemopped und zuletzt hab' ich noch mein refrigerator defrosted. Die Mrs. Johnson sagt ich sollt' mich nich' so strainen, denn dasz gibt ein' high blood-pressure."

"*He studied and makes good grades. And he helps me too with housework. This morning I borrowed Mrs. Johnson's vacuum cleaner and cleaned the rugs. Then I mopped the whole house, and finally I defrosted the refrigerator. Mrs. Johnson says I shouldn't strain myself so, because that gives high blood pressure,*" Ruby Jean explained.

95

Emma thought of her own chores. Taking care of the chickens, a vegetable garden, separating milk by hand, making butter, managing an old house with no running water, no electricity, not even a kerosene range in the kitchen . . . . There was sometimes a little time left for her to sew or mend.

"Wie likest du dein job—*How do you like your job?*" she asked.

"Oh, der is' fine," Ruby Jean answered proudly. "Der boss von der hosiery mill bezahlt sure gute salaries. Mit den Geld was der Charlie von den govuh'ment kriegt fier drausen im machine shop arbeiten haben mir immer plenty. Der Charlie is' sure gut zu mich," the young wife said dreamily.

"Oh, it's fine. The boss from the hosiery mill sure pays good salaries. With the money Charlie gets from the government for working out in the machine shop, I always have plenty. Charlie is sure good to me."

Seeing her daughter's happiness made Emma glad she had consented to the girl's taking a job as housemaid in the home of one of the officers at Randolph Field. It was there she had met Charlie O'Connell, and he seemed to have made her a good husband.

"Die Marjorie Fichtner hat letzte Woch' ein' Jung' aus Seguin geheirat'. Die haben 'ne grosze wedding celebration bei der Sattler Halle gehabt. Wie ich die Frau Werner beim Ernte Fest in Anhalt geseh'n hab' hat sie mir gesagt die hätten vier verschiedene Sorten sandwiches und allerlei cookies gehabt," Emma continued, hoping to arouse Ruby Jean's interest in her former friends.

"Last week Marjoie Fichtner married a boy from Seguin. They had a big wedding celebration at Sattler Hall. When I saw Mrs. Werner at the Harvest Fest in Anhalt, she told me they had four different kinds of sandwiches and all kinds of cookies."

"Well, that's that," the girl said as she shelved the last dish, ignoring her mother's story. "Let's go into the living room and visit."

Once in the presence of the men, the women had little opportunity to say anything. Secretly each was thankful, because their attempts at conversation had thus far been almost completely unsuccessful.

Emma could hear the dull thud which Leroy's baseball made as it struck the outside of the wall against which the boy was tossing it rhythmically. At least he spent Saturday nights and Sundays on the farm with them, so that she still had some time in which to keep him from becoming a complete stranger to his parents. Sometimes she wondered whether Heinrich had not been right in discouraging his continuing his schooling. She felt certain the boy would never want to farm for a living, and they could not afford to educate him, even for a trade.

"What do you all think about this idea of drafting fellows for a year of army training?" Charlie asked. Charlie's own stand on the question was rather obvious though unstated since he had enlisted in the army voluntarily years ago and was apparently more than pleased with his situation.

"It looks to me like we are just asking for trouble, with the war going on in Europe and all," Heinrich said. He had escaped draft in the first World War because his aging father had needed him on the farm, but he remembered what had happened to some of the young men he had known.

Emma thought only that Leroy's future would perhaps be forcibly taken out of their hands, and his.

"A lot of country boys will have a chance to get around and see things like they never would have any other way," Ruby Jean offered with a glib callousness of which only the very thoughtless are capable.

"Why don't we all ride down to Ma's Cafe and have a bottle of beer?" Charlie suggested, trying to shift the conversation away from the disagreeable.

Before Emma had a chance to object, they were half-way out to the car. Leroy took possession of the steering-wheel, while Emma, Ruby Jean, and Charlie got in the back seat. Heinrich, aware that his son was a more efficient motorist than he himself could ever be, restrained himself from giving advice.

The little cafe was crowded with country people who had taken a recess from their shopping in order to get some refreshment. The proprietress, a large, jovial woman, and her helpers were kept more than busy taking and filling orders. Above the clatter of dishes and buzz of voices one could hear occasional strains of a polka from the jukebox.

Charlie headed for one oilcloth-covered table near the window, and the rest followed and took their seats. A round of beer was ordered and consumed without conversational accompaniment. Leroy was sent down the street to the blacksmith's to call for the sharpened plowshares while Heinrich entered a conversation with one of his friends at a nearby table. Now and then one of the young people would greet one of their contemporaries whose presence had just been noticed. Though she knew almost everyone there by first name, Emma scarcely more than acknowledged the friendly greetings with a quiet smile. She would have liked to show off her new dress to some of the women, but then she remembered what her daughter had said about it. She would have enjoyed the exchange of the latest news from the various parts of the county, but she realized she would have little to contribute. So she just sat sipping the glass of beer while all around her was the gaiety which only a group of people who work hard all week can generate on a Saturday afternoon.

Across the street in front of the Voelker home, a breeze was prodding the first yellowing leaves of the season off the white oak and chasing them down the street. The white frame Victorian building looked flat like a painted canvas stage-set against a backdrop of rosy sky.

If Heinrich had not returned just then and suggested they leave, Emma would have taken it upon herself to do so. She wanted to get out into the fresh air, away from the sour smell of the beer and the nasal tones from the music box droning, "I don't worry, 'cause it makes no diff'rence now."

When they reached Ruby Jean's little house, the three young people got out.

"I'm not going along home," Leroy announced. "One of the boys at school got me a date, and we are going to Echo Hall to the dance," he stated, as if this weren't the first time he would be taking out a girl and the first time he would not spend Sunday with his parents.

Emma was silent, and Heinrich offered no word of protest. He actually seemed pleased and amused by the boy's suddenly developed interest in the opposite sex. It wasn't that which saddened Emma. It was the realization that he should prefer to stay in town the one day in the week he could be at home. He should have known how much it meant to her to have him with her on Sundays. Young people always felt there was so much time left. But *was* there? Emma thought.

"Have a good time, then," she finally said, wishing Heinrich would hurry and get underway before her feelings betrayed her.

"Macht's gut—*So long!*" Heinrich called as he waved goodbye.

Neither uttered a word until they were well outside town. Heinrich tapped the bowl of his pipe against the window frame as if it were a miniature gavel with which he was rapping for attention.

"Der Mueller hat gesagt sie wirden eine high-line dicht an uns vorbei legen. Die ganze Gegend kann dann rural electrification haben. Winsch' sure wir kennten's afforden, aber das kostet su viel Geld."

"Mueller said they're going to lay a highline right by us. Then the whole area can have rural electrification. Sure hope we can afford it, but it costs too much money."

Emma looked down at her large, work-weary hands, which even in the flattering twilight looked coarse and sun-browned.

"Oh, well, das hat ja noch Zeit—*there's still time for that,*" she said, trying to convince herself that someday . . . but tomorrow she had to finish weeding the garden, mend some clothing, and help Heinrich repair the fence by the creek. Yes, tomorrow would be another busy day.

Wild-fire

1944

From his observation point on the top of the cliff, Fred Bracht heard the explosion and watched the wall of lime-stone a quarter of a mile away crumble and collapse onto the floor of the quarry pit with a loud crash. After a few moments the avalanche stopped and the dust settled lightly on the massive boulders. Satisfied with the result of the carefully planned blast, Fred lighted a cigar and set out in his dusty little coupe for home and supper.

As he drove past the group of buildings which formed the crushed-stone plant, he waved to the workers of the day shift who had assembled there after loading the blast. Slowly the men collected their lunch pails and piled into the waiting truck in which they would be taken into town. For fifteen minutes the heavy vehicle rumbled over the cement highway, bouncing each time it crossed one of the joints in the cement.

The men in the back of the truck were not disturbed by being jostled about so roughly. Tomorrow was Cinco de Mayo, the Mexican independence day, and all of them were thinking and talking about the dance which would be held that night at the Salón del Gallo. Tomorrow would be a holiday. Pío Quinto Gutiérrez was saying there would be fireworks and dancing and music. Mucha musica! Señor Martin Kreutz had sold the committee some *cabritos* which Ramón Zamora, the undertaker, who was also a very good cook, had consented to barbecue. There would be food and fun for everybody at the city park. They had tried to get permission to use Landa Park, but the excuse had been given that a group of soldiers from Ft. Sam Houston had already reserved the picnic grounds for that day.

"¿Quién es la reina de la fiesta—*Who is the queen of the festival?*" one of the older men inquired.

"Mi hermana, Estéfana—*My sister, Stephanie*," one young fellow answered proudly, his white-toothed smile gleaming. "Es *muy* bonita, é inteligente, también—*She is very pretty, and intelligent also.*"

"No muy semejante á su hermano, ¿verdad?—*She is not similar to her brother, right?*" the blond man next to him commented, administering a friendly slap on the shoulder of the victim of his teasing. All the men were laughing heartily in good-natured amusement as the truck stopped just inside the border of the town to deposit some of its occupants.

After a second stop had been made in the town square, the truck drove on across the bridge and through the precinct known as Comal Town. Though neat and well-constructed, the houses in this section were cheaper for the most part than those on the other side of the river. Here and there a cow was staked out to graze on an empty lot, and chickens fluttered excitedly across the streets when an automobile approached. Each house had a mailbox on its gatepost with a name and R. F. D. #1 lettered in black upon its side, and in some of the back yards were outdoor privies. Everywhere there were gardens, not only because the residents preferred a semi-rural existence, but also because the soil was the best in the town for cultivation.

Soon the truck made its third stop in the center of a little colony of frame cubicles which were set upon bare cedar posts. As soon as all the remaining passengers had scrambled out, the driver drove on across the tracks, through the newest and most homogeneously luxurious residential addition of the town, then circled back to the business district.

From the porches of some of the huts women called to their menfolk. Barefooted children who were playing in the streets mingled with their returning fathers and brothers, who, after exchanging brief goodbyes, dispersed in various directions.

Jesús Cantú left the paved street after walking along it for two blocks and turned onto the narrower graveled road. Though he could not yet see his house from there, the thin stream of smoke rising from its chimney was visible above the tops of the trees in the ravine ahead. The one-room house in which the Cantús lived was set back about a hundred yards from the road. It was a drab, unpainted shack which appeared to have dropped carelessly on the slope from extreme fatigue. To get to it, Jesús walked across the bed of a dry creek, then trudged up the embankment on the other side. Two milk goats, bleating plaintively, were tied to trees at a safe distance from a sagging clothesline, on which a woman's petticoat, a tiny pair of rompers, and a faded work shirt were hung. On the narrow porch of the house an old woman stood watering several potted plants from a rusty tin-can which looked as if someone had stepped on it to give it a spout. As the man came up to the steps of the house, he greeted the old woman.

"¿Cómo le va, mamacita?"

"Muy bien, Jesús," his mother-in-law answered, removing from her shrunken mouth the pipe she was smoking.

At the sound of the voices a little girl of about ten came to the open door. Straddling her right hip was her little brother, who was not yet able to walk. The baby wore only a diaper which showed that both he and the floor of the house had been somewhat neglected. His sister was clothed in a faded yellow percale dress, and the two braided loops of her dark hair were bound together with a red satin bow which was partly untied. At the sight of her father, the girl smiled broadly and went over to him.

"¿Cómo le va, niña?" the man asked, laying his hand on the child's thin shoulder. Almost convulsively she grasped his hand. It was a warm greeting, although the girl did not say a word.

Every word was an obstacle for little Lupe Cantú. She had been born with a malformed palate which impeded her speech to such a great extent that scarcely anything she said was intelligible. As a consequence she spoke only when it was absolutely necessary, relying otherwise on gestures and facial expressions to make herself understood. And her intelligent black eyes in the strong Indian bone structure of her face were eloquent as they told her father that she was glad that he was home. Then, at the bidding of her mother, she beckoned Jesús and her grandmother into the house, where the family sat down to their evening meal of tortillas, frijoles, and warm goat milk.

Amalie Bracht had heard the distant thunder of the explosion and had known that her husband would soon be home from work. The food having been prepared earlier, Amalie and her eldest daughter, Johanne, then started to set the table for supper. Meanwhile, Annalies, the only other child who was still under the parental roof, was brought home in an automobile by one of her fellow teachers. As always, she went directly to the bathroom to scrub her hands with strong disinfectant soap before touching anything in the house. When she came into the kitchen, her mother asked, "Well, how was the day, Liesel?"

"Worse than usual," Annalies answered dejectedly. "Tomorrow is a holiday, and I couldn't get any attention from the children all day."

Annalies had taken the job in the Mexican school because of the war-time shortage of teachers. Originally she had been prompted by a feeling of responsibility to her hometown, but eight months of being pent up in a room with a group of dirty, undisciplined children had somewhat shattered her altruism. How could she hope to interest children in improving their minds when their diets, except for the noon meal which the school cafeteria served, were terribly deficient. When a little girl steals chalk crayons from the schoolroom because she does not possess a single toy, one cannot convince her that she has done a wrong. If a hubcap disappears from a teacher's automobile because a hungry boy knows what it is worth in terms of candy, punishment only increases the resentment he has stored in his heart. A genteel young woman who has always had a room of her own can scarcely understand the problem of the boy who writes obscenities on the restroom wall because he has slept all his life in the same room with his entire family.

Amalie Bracht was actually glad to see Annalies' discouragement. Let someone else teach the Mexican children. Her daughter did not need the money, and she feared the girl's health was suffering from the experience.

"Mama, the school nurse came over today and washed all the children's heads with kerosene again. I'm so sick at the stomach from that odor that I don't think I can eat a thing," Annalies continued.

Amalie gave her youngest daughter a compassionate look but set a place for her at the table just the same, thinking that she would develop an appetite once she saw the attractive cold supper her mother and sister had prepared.

In a few moments Fred Bracht drove into the back yard, and Johanne went out to brush the lime dust off his clothes before he came indoors. After greeting his wife and daughters, he went to wash up for supper. When he returned to the dining room his aging face looked healthy and contented though tired.

"Every time we blast at the quarry nowadays I thank my lucky stars that that new kind of dynamite was invented," he said. "Remember those awful headaches I used to have when we used the old kind?"

"I should say I do!" Amalie exclaimed, marveling at the mellowness which Fred had developed as he grew older. She had never given much credence to his notions of what caused the severe headaches he had suffered from, since she herself was convinced they had been caused by worrying.

"We aren't going to operate the plant tomorrow, because all the Mexicans are going to celebrate Cinco de Mayo. I don't suppose you have to work either tomorrow, Liesel?" Fred asked.

"No, I don't Papa. I thought I'd lounge around all day and get some rest for a change," Annalies said feebly while toying with her food.

"A day in the sunshine would do you more good I think," her father commented, looking at his daughter's pale complexion and tired eyes. He was determined not to try to influence his youngest child to give up her work, but he hoped with all his heart that she would do so of her own free will. He knew how futile it was for one lone person to try to help the underprivileged with neither their own cooperation nor that of the other people of the town. Again and again he had tried it with the men who worked under him and had failed each time. It was too big a job for a handful of people, and all but a few did not care at all about what happened to the "greasers" until their own welfare was affected. Instead they complained of the flagrance of the young Mexicans, who loafed on street corners while their own sons had to go into the army. Few stopped to realize that their own sons were healthy, whereas the Mexican youths had not been able to pass the army physical examination because of undernourishment and disease.

"I thought perhaps we could spend the day on the farms," Fred suggested. "We could have a sort of picnic. I could see how everything is getting along out there, and you all could have a nice, quiet day to do as you please."

It was agreed that they would drive to the farm rather early before the sun got very hot. After the women had done the dishes and Fred had listened to the news broadcast, they all retired to their rooms to get a good night's sleep.

From long-established habit, Fred Bracht rose early the next morning and dressed quietly in order not to wake his family. Softly he walked down the stairs and flung open the windows to let the cool morning air into the stuffy rooms on the first floor of the house. After carrying in the bottles of milk which had been deposited on the doorstep, he went for his morning walk. Every morning a group of the early risers of the neighborhood met at the post office, where they went to get their mail. Fred greeted the other people, who were standing about reading or chatting in groups of two or three.

Dr. Roy MacMillan and Sheriff Scheel were standing together under the clock against the wall as Fred came up to unlock his box.

"You're just the man I want to see," the sheriff said as Fred approached.

"Yes? What can I do for you?" he asked.

"There has been an accident out at the Six Shooter Ranch," Dr. MacMillan declared. "One of the Mexican huts burned, and a baby was killed. The other child was not critically injured. Fortunately the Comal Town fire crew got there before a great deal of damage was done, and they called me when they saw that a doctor was needed."

"Have you any idea how the fire started?" Fred Bracht asked.

"Yes," the sheriff answered, lowering his voice. "We know there was an explosion of some sort. The house is so near the old quarry, where some government contractors are getting stone, that I wonder if it was exactly an accident."

"What in the world are you driving at?" Fred inquired incredulously. "You can't think that someone deliberately tried to blow up a worthless little shack and injure a couple of innocent children!"

"No, I don't think they intended to blow up the house," the sheriff continued. "But there is some valuable machinery right in that area, and the material from the quarry is being used to build a new military highway not far from here."

"The sheriff thinks it might have been an attempt at sabotage," Roy MacMillan explained quietly.

Fred Bracht could scarcely believe his ears. "Look, sheriff, I know a little about explosives myself. I've been working with them for almost thirty years. And let me tell you, they do just about what you want them to do if you know how to handle them, and nobody would be fool enough to handle them without knowing how to control the results. You agree the house was not the object of the destruction. I say it was an accident in the full sense of the word."

"Okay, Mr. Bracht," the officer of the law agreed half-heartedly. "But I have to look into the cause, and I'd appreciate your help."

"Certainly," Fred answered. "Pick me up at my home in about an hour, and I'll go with you. I suggest you come along, Roy. We can use whatever information you can contribute."

Shortly before noon, after Fred, the sheriff, and the doctor had been examining the environs of the accident for several hours, the sheriff summarized their finding.

"This much we know: there was an explosion, as Dr. MacMillan says the baby's corpse shows. Also there were open flames, as indicated by the appearance of the interior of the house and type of burns the children sustained. Kerosene from the lamp was spilled on the table top and on the floor, where, consequently, the fire did the most damage. Had the lamp exploded, the liquid would have been sprayed about over a greater area, and the glass would have been broken into smaller fragments. Probably the girl overturned the lamp and set the house on fire. But what exploded?" The sheriff thrust his hands into his pockets as if to punctuate his perplexity.

"If the blast had been caused by dynamite, the house would have been leveled to the ground," Fred Bracht said calmly. "Besides, none of the dynamite from any of the powder magazines in this vicinity is missing. You said you had investigated that yourself, sheriff."

The sheriff nodded. "Let's examine the house once

more," he said, "and then I will go and question the family again."

The men walked up onto the porch, where the potted plants still stood on the wooded railing as if nothing had happened. The inside of the house bespoke with dreadful clarity the poverty of its occupants. The walls were covered with brittle, smoky newspapers which had been glued there years earlier. The furnishings consisted of the remains of a burned table, three rickety straight chairs, a badly charred rocker with one of its runners gone, two iron cots, and a small wood stove. Under the beds were several boxes containing all the family's clothing and two old serapes which were used as blankets. On an unburned wall hung a two-year old calendar with a smoke-stained picture of the Blessed Virgin on it. A window was cut into each of the three walls, the fourth wall being the side from which one entered the house. There were neither curtains nor wire screens, and one window pane had been replaced by a small sheet of the same type of corrugated tin which formed the roof of the hut.

The three men again carefully searched the entire room for clues to the mysterious explosion, but found nothing of importance for which they had not previously accounted. Reluctantly the sheriff agreed that they return to town to eat and continue the investigation later.

Amalie Bracht warmed the food left over from dinner for her husband when he returned to his home, distressed and downcast by the sadness of the situation which had been occupying his thought for the past hours. He had always felt a great pity for people who lived in such squalor, but had never been able to alter their condition appreciably. What if their wages were raised a little? There was always a new mouth to feed to counterbalance any increase in the family's income. What if the children did go to school and learn to read and write English? They were still almost limited to being housemaids and day laborers or farm hands. Only a few managed to set themselves up as shoemakers, or fruit peddlers, or get jobs as janitors in one of the public buildings. Even if one taught the younger generation the rudiments of hygiene, they went home at night to insect-infected huts with no plumbing and slept in the same room with their tuberculous or syphilitic parents. No one cared whether the sewer lines were extended until a case of typhoid turned up among the "whites." And when a Mexican was killed or permanently maimed, the poor wretches were berated for their ignorance and carelessness.

"People have been telephoning all morning wanting to know if the saboteur has been caught yet," Amalie was saying. "It seems someone overheard you and the sheriff talking this morning in the post office about the explosion."

"Good Lord!" Fred Bracht exclaimed in disgust.

Amalie went on to tell about the telephone conversations she had had since Fred had left with the sheriff. Mrs. Weber remembered hearing over the radio that several German prisoners of war had escaped from a camp in northern Texas and were thought to be heading for the Mexican border. That would land them right through this town, so that they might have been responsible for the explosion. Some believed that the saboteur would have had to be well acquainted with the premises. That was why Agnes Heimer decided it was probably old Johannes Voelker, who had a farm just across from the scene of the explosion. Did Amalie recall whether he had ever received his final citizenship papers? Mrs. Webb, the Baptist minister's wife, told Julie Schrauber that she thought probably Jesús Cantú had set the house on fire himself. You know how drunk those Mexicans get when they celebrate.

"It seems nothing has quite as much appeal as an unexplained tragedy," Fred commented. "I guess everybody likes to play at being a sleuth."

"Oh, but those aren't half the versions of what happened," Amalie declared. "Mr. Matthews—he's that new young man who works for the paper, you know—wants me to tell you not to ignore the possibility that someone might have set the house on fire to 'sow seeds of dissension' between the gringos and the Mexicans. Nazis always work on the principle of divide and conquer, he says. And Mary Williams thinks maybe the Mexican has been stealing dynamite from the quarry and storing it in his house. Her husband said Jesús Cantú was originally a 'wet-back' who had been returned to Mexico and later was permitted to re-enter the United States. He contends that a man who is capable of one illegal action wouldn't hesitate to commit another."

"The acoustics in the post office certainly must be good. None of those people were in the building when I was talking with the sheriff this morning, but they seem to know much more than we do about what happened," Fred said sarcastically. He was incensed that news of a tragic accident should be dramatized by idle minds for entertainment. "I'm willing to bet that we never find out what occurred. What's done is done. I can't see what the sheriff expects to accomplish by asking the family all those questions. The adults were at the celebration at the Salón del Gallo when the accident happened. Old Johannes Voelker, who lived across the road, saw the flames, telephoned the fire department, took the children over to his house, and called the doctor. The little girl can't speak distinctly enough to explain what happened, if she knows it at all, which I doubt. As for sabotage, the idea is ridiculous. But people won't accept an explanation which doesn't appeal to their imaginations."

A week passed, and the town stopped talking about the explosion, because, although the sheriff could not explain the accident, it seemed quite evident that there had been no foul play involved. The Cantú baby was buried with the customary ceremony, and the remaining members of the family moved in with relatives until their own house could be repaired. Jesús went back to his job at the quarry, and little Lupe returned to her desk in school.

It was the day before classes would be dismissed for the summer vacation, and the children were restless, although Annalies Bracht tried to keep them occupied. During the afternoon she decided she would have the children write a composition just to keep the class quiet and orderly.

"Lupe not have a pencil," said a boy who was the self-appointed warden of the afflicted child's welfare.

Annalies searched in her desk-drawer and brought out a small mechanical pencil which her father had given her for her birthday some years before. Then she walked back to where Lupe sat and offered the pencil to the child. At the sight of the small metal cylinder, the girl screamed in terror, covered her ears with her hands, and ran out of the door.

After asking the school principal to keep her class for her, the young teacher went outside to look for Lupe. The child was sitting under a tree behind the school, still with her hands over her ears and screaming, "Encendio! Encendio!" in her strange distorted way.

Suddenly the cause of the child's fear was obvious to Annalies. She took the mechanical pencil from her pocket and examined it again. Yes, it looked *very* much like a cartridge, only longer. More like a blasting cap. She had often seen pictures of them in advertisements in her father's trade journals. Of course! The child had thought the pencil was a blasting cap and had associated it with fire.

Carefully Annalies replaced the pencil into her pocket in order not to frighten the child further. She spoke softly and soothingly until the little girl stopped crying and wiped her nose with the hem of her dress.

Calmly Annalies began to recount her version of what had happened the night of the fire. Sometimes she would use Spanish words when the child seemed not to understand the English. Now and then the little girl would interrupt her with gestures, and Annalies would revise the story until it checked with the child's memories. By and by what had happened became clear.

The adults had gone to the dance at the Salón del Gallo and had left Lupe at home with the baby. Sometime later she had sat down in the rocking chair by the table to read her lessons. Her little brother had been playing on the floor beside her. Looking up from the book, she had noticed that the little boy was playing with a small metal stick. She supposed it had dropped from her father's work clothes which hung over the back of the chair. When she had tried to take it away from the baby, the cartridge had rolled across the floor and she had accidentally rocked across it with the chair. She had been thrown out of the chair, and the kerosene lamp had fallen off the table and started the fire. Almost immediately after the fire started, Señor Voelker had come over to take them to his house.

When Annalies had finished piecing together the story, Lupe began to weep again, but this time as if she were greatly relieved to have shared the knowledge of her hideous experience. The school bell rang, and children burst out of all the doors to head for their homes.

"Go get your books, Lupe," Annalies said gently. "I'll go find someone to take you home."

When Annalies went into the classroom to tell Lupe that the principal would take her home in his car, she found only a note in childish handwriting lying on her desk. Unfolding it she read:

Dear Miss Bracht,
I tell you sooner what happen, but I know my father- he get fired when Mr. Bracht find out he take this thing from quory. My father no know he have any- thing in his pockets. Pleese tell your father my father no want to steel, not hurt nobody. My father is good man, like your father.

Lupe Cantú

Annalies folded the paper and put it into her handbag. All the way home she was haunted by the vision of the poor afflicted child trying to study her lessons by the light of a kerosene lamp in that tinder-box of a hovel. How different it was from her own room with its gaily flowered wall- paper and frilly curtains and carefully engineered electric illumination! Yet the child had the same strong love and admiration for her father which she, Annalies, had for hers. It was a penetrating thought and one not easily dismissed.

When Fred Bracht read the note, he was profoundly touched. "I think Jesús Cantú has suffered more than his penalty already," he said.

Twilight

Neu Braunfels, Texas
the 20. February, 1945

*M*y dear friend Renner!

The doctor has advised that I keep myself as quiet as possible, at least until I recover entirely from the attacks of dizziness which have resulted from my illness. Even the automobile rides which I am in the habit of taking with my son, Friedrich, are considered too strenuous. Since we shall not for a while be able to visit one another as formerly, I have decided that I shall write you, not just to pass the long hours of inactivity which burden me, but also to continue a comradeship which I have valued for these many years.

Everyone is very kind. Friedrich spends time with me

when he can and manages my few affairs for me. His wife, Amalie, sees to it that Fräulein Lambert keeps my household as nearly as possible as it was kept before my wife died. In short, I am cared for like the fragile old relic that I am.

Two of my old bad habits I have been permitted to retain, though to a greatly limited extent. I am allowed a package of cigarettes and one glass of wine each day. Just twenty cigarettes and one glass of wine which a child could drink without stimulating effect!

My son, Robert, frequently sends me new books from Milwaukee, since fortunately my eyes still do me service. Recently he sent me a new Goethe biography, which I am finding very interesting. I have always preferred Schiller to Goethe, however, partly because the latter turned the heads of so many fine young women without marrying any of them. He finally married a woman of low station when their son was about twenty years old. Those are not the actions of a man of honor.

It is my sincere wish that you may soon be well enough to pay me a visit, so that we may resume the conversations which have always been so stimulating to

Your old friend,
Gustav Bracht

~

Neu Braunfels, Texas
the 24. February, 1945

My dear friend Bracht!

Your letter I was very glad to receive, and I think a correspondence would be the best possible substitute for our customary frequent visits which I have grown to miss greatly since circumstances have forced us to discontinue them. My doctor, who is himself no longer a young man, has not yet attained the age at which old friends become doubly precious because of their increasing scarcity. Consequently, he limits my activities greatly in the hope of restoring my former energy which at our stage of life is rarely retrievable.

In the last issue of the *Neu Braunfelser Zeitung* I read that although Köln has been heavily bombed, the cathedral still stands. I remember very clearly your telling me how tremendously impressed you were upon seeing it for the first time when you and a fellow student made a journey there from Bonn. Having grown up almost in its shadow, I am, of course, as attached to it as a Parisian to the Eiffel Tower or a New Yorker to the lights of Broadway. But the Germany we knew as boys, I fear, is not destined to outlast us.

Once when I was teaching in one of the county schools, I was asked by one of my older students to which of the differences between Germany and America I had found it most difficult to accustom myself. Without hesitation I knew the answer. In America everything is replaced almost as soon as it begins to show signs of age, whereas in Europe age is generally cause for veneration. America is youth's paradise, and I am old. But life in Texas has adequate compensations to offer. Almost everyone has room for gardens and the air is clear and healthful. I feel sure I could not now survive a winter in Europe, where I recall having spent long, impatient months indoors awaiting the spring when we could again make occasional excursions to the *Volksgarten.*

My wife is calling me to supper, so I must end this letter which I hope will find you in improving health.

Your old friend,
Ferdinand Renner

Neu Braunfels, Texas
the 3. March, 1945

My dear friend Renner!

An annoying recurrence of my illness has prevented my answering your much appreciated letter sooner. The resumption of our visits which I had anticipated so hopefully must unfortunately again be delayed.

One day while I was confined to bed, Amalie, the wife of my son, Friedrich, came to help Fräulein Lambert bottle the agarita wine which I had made before sugar was rationed. It has turned out to be a delicious light red wine which compares favorably with any I have ever tasted. At the first opportunity I shall send you some so that you may know that I am not making false claims for my "product."

After the ladies had finished their work, my daughter-in-law read to me from the *Zeitung*. As a comparative "newcomer" to the town you may not know that this is the oldest German newspaper in the state and has always been affectionately known by the older subscribers as "die Tante—*the auntie*." When Herr Oheim (literally, *Uncle*) took over the editorship, ample use was made of the opportunity to joke about the amusing combination of the two names.

Among the passages which Amalie read to me was an excerpt from a recent novel based on the history of the German immigration into Texas in the years immediately after 1844. The book is being printed by the *Zeitung* in serial form and is a most beautiful account of the great trials and disappointments with which the settlers met before succeeding in their plan to establish colonies where the ideals which had caused them to leave their fatherland could materialize. As a son of two of those pioneers I may be inclined to be more impressed by such a story than its literary merits warrant. However, I feel that you too will enjoy reading it if you find the time.

One can tell that spring is nearly here, because all the air smells of mountain laurel. When we lived on the farm my wife frequently complained of headaches which she attributed to the strong fragrance of the beautiful violet-colored blossoms of this shrub which paint the hills each year at this time. Since that was long before allergies or hay fever were recognized as legitimate ailments, I was always openly skeptical about her theories. Dear, noble woman! How faithfully and uncomplainingly she stood by me for over fifty years! You are fortunate to have your life companion still with you as your world grows smaller. My own grows continually emptier and more limited, and each of your letters represents a happy interruption of the monotony of my days.

Devotedly, your
Gustav Bracht

~

Neu Braunfels, Texas
the 12. March, 1945

My dear friend Bracht!

Your calling me a "'newcomer' to the town" amused me greatly and shows that even in your illness your sense of humor has not deserted you. As you know I have lived within a few miles of this town for over sixty years, forty of which I spent as the master of the same little country school. I lived to see a number of my former students become trustees of that school, and in some cases I taught three generations of the same family.

It was here that I met and married my wife, whose steadfastness and spirit have many times kept me from losing courage. Yesterday she took me by the arm and led me across the street to see Frau Wenzel's rose vines. One of them has seventy-two pink blossoms, and when I paid the woman a compliment upon her ability as a gardener, her eyes were bright with pride. How little it takes to give happiness, and how often we neglect our opportunities to bring others joy! Certainly your letters and the kindnesses of my family and neighbors have frequently lifted me out of the depression into which my physical incapacity has settled me.

As a Rheinlander I consider myself something of a connoisseur of wines, and that which you sent me is truly delicious. I am saving most of it in the hope that the doctor will permit me to celebrate my approaching birthday with a large family gathering. Such affairs always give me a sense of contentment and well-being which nothing else can provide, although there are always two whose absence is acutely felt. I am not certain which was the more tormenting: the finality of the news of my youngest son's death when the commercial airplane which he was flying crashed some years ago, or the uncertainty of the report "missing in action" which was recently received of my grandson whose bomber did not return from a mission over Germany. Most tragic of all, perhaps, is the hatred of all things German which the young wife is cultivating in the small son because of the fate which has befallen his father.

When my daughter delivers this letter, I shall have her bring you some of the *Kaffeetorte* which she and my wife baked this morning. The recipe is one which Frau Bracht once gave my wife, who sends you this little gift in appreciation of your help in preserving the good cheer of

Your old friend,
Ferdinand Renner

Neu Braunfels, Texas
the 21. March, 1945

My dear friend Renner!

The cake which Frau Renner so kindly sent had a short life span, because I demanded a piece of it with every meal and with my afternoon wine. Baking is the one phase of household work in which Fräulein Lambert cannot simulate the excellence of my wife.

I am told that the tornado which struck Landa Park a day ago greatly damaged the beautiful old oaks. Strange that the storm should have visited the very spot where the immigrants first set up camp, and on the eve of the centennial of the founding of the town. As you probably know, the Austrian flag was raised at the Sophienburg (which was then a kind of log fortress) on Good Friday, just one hundred years ago today.

I think the plan to postpone the celebration of the anniversary until the young men of the town return from the war is a good one, since it is the young people who most need to be reminded of the valour of their ancestors. They should be made aware that their forefathers were the first citizens in Texas to tax themselves for the establishment of a public free school, and that "equal opportunity for all" was to them not merely an empty phrase but a *Weltanschauung*. Most of all, they should be encouraged to appreciate how peculiarly equipped they are to do a job which, it appears, will soon be theirs to do: to show the world that democratic ideas and Germanic blood are not incompatible.

It seems that one must grow helpless and unproductive before one realizes fully that only that which is planted at the right season and carefully tended can ever bear fruit and scatter seed. Most of my life I have been too busy plowing and planting to give much time to philosophizing, and now that is about all for which I have sufficient strength.

Write me when you are able, and convey to the thoughtful Frau Renner the best wishes of her appreciative friend and yours,

Gustav Bracht

~

Neu Braunfels, Texas
the 2. April, 1945

My dear friend Bracht!

My eighty-fifth birthday was one of the most pleasant I can recall, although I was forced to spend it very quietly. My sons and their families were able to come from Friedrichsburg and San Antonio, so that the dining room table had to be extended to its full length for the evening meal. After nightfall, the Concordia singing society, which I directed for many years, surprised me with a very nice serenade. One of the outstanding treats was the rendition of my favorite old song, "Aus der Jugendzeit," by your grand-daughter, Johanne. She is one of the youngest members of the organization and certainly its leading soprano. The voice she must have inherited from the Kreutz side, for you, my dear Bracht, could never carry a tune even when the wine was plentiful and good. Nevertheless, I always wished you would join one of the local singing societies. One of the greatest sources of enjoyment to me, especially as I grow old, is the annual Sängerfest. There, over a glass of beer or two, one can talk with old friends from the hill country and Austin and San Antonio, and sing together just for the pleasure of singing and refreshing the memory. The old songs are still the best!

My daughter gave me a number of beautiful phonograph recordings to add to our collection. One of these is the "Akademische Festovertüre" which I have always counted among my favorites. Its two closing themes are taken from student songs which are intimately associated in my mind with my university days at Jena. And what glorious days they were! In the late '70s it looked very much as though Germany would finally take its place among the most respected nations of the world, and all the young men of the land were fired with new enthusiasm for liberalism.

Although I am not strong, I can complain neither of pain nor of real discomfort. Perhaps if the weather continues to be clear I may be permitted to begin to visit with you again soon. Looking forward to that day, I am

Your devoted friend
Ferdinand Renner

∼

Neu Braunfels, Texas
the 15. April, 1945

My dear friend Renner!

The news of the president's death was certainly startling. I have never been one of his supporters, but the charm and power of his personality cannot be denied. It will be interesting to see whether the new president will be able to fill the shoes of his predecessor, whose aristocratic manner and oratorical ability accounted for many of his successes.

On Wednesday my grand-daughter, Elsbeth, brought her child up for a visit with me. They are staying here with Friedrich and Amalie while James Wilson, the little girl's father, awaits embarkation in New York. The child is quite beautiful and bears a strong resemblance to my wife when she was young. Like most of the young people nowadays, Elsbeth has forgotten almost all the German she knew, and the child, Linda, speaks only English. I have no doubt that in a few years very little German will be spoken here.

Already the schools no longer include it in their curricula, and only the two large churches have German services once weekly, I am told.

You say that Johanne must have inherited her musical talent from her mother. On the contrary, my friend, I think she inherited it from my father's family. When I was in the university at Bonn, I frequently went to Aachen to visit with my paternal relatives, two of whom were in grand opera. They were an amusing lot, with their educated tastes and undisciplined temperaments. It was a strange setting for a poor Texas boy to drop into. My father, who was a lawyer, died shortly after the Civil War, and my mother had to teach school to support her large family. Only her remarkable frugality made it possible for her to educate us, yet all but two of us attended college.

Fräulein Lambert has served notice that she will leave at the end of the month to join her widowed sister whose son has been reported killed in action. Consequently I shall have to make other arrangements for my care. My health is not improving as I had hoped it might, but a visit from you would, as always, give me much pleasure.

Auf Wiedersehen!

Your old friend,
Gustav Bracht

~

Neu Braunfels, Texas
the 9. May, 1945

My dear Herr Renner!

My family has asked me to write and tell you of the death of my grandfather, your old friend, at six o'clock yesterday morning. Two weeks ago Grossvater suffered another stroke and was unconscious except for a few moments at a time thereafter. During one of those short periods of consciousness, he directed me to send you his volume of Theodor Fontane's poems, which accompanies this letter.

A few hours later we heard the news that the war in Europe is over. Having been informed that your grandson who was listed as missing is alive and well, you must be greatly relieved. But as a native German, you must have received the news of the Allied victory with mixed feelings, as did we. I have known Germany only as a child who holds a seashell to its ear knows and loves the ocean he has never seen.

Our grief at Grossvater's death is greatly softened by the knowledge that his was a full and useful life, a consolation which the sorrowing families of many young men do not have on this day.

Extending the best wishes of my family to you and Frau Renner, I am

Respectfully yours,
Annalies Bracht

Ferdinand Renner laid the letter aside with trembling hands and opened the accompanying book where the little red satin ribbon divided its crisp, thin pages, and read:

Ob unsre Jungen, in ihrem Erdreisten,
Wirklich was besseres schaffen und leisten,
Ob dem Parnasse sie näher gekommen,
Oder blosz einen Maulwurfshügel erklommen,
Ob sie, mit andern Neusittenverfechtern,
Die Menschheit bessern oder verschlechtern,
Ob sie Frieden sän oder Sturm entfachen,
Ob sie Himmel oder Hölle machen ———
Eins läszt sie stehn auf siegreichem Grunde:
Sie haben den Tag, sie haben die Stunde;

Der Mohr kann gehn, neu Spiel hebt an,
Sie beherrschen die Szene, sie sind dran.

Is the youth of today with rebellious zeal
Creating, achieving something better and real?
Have they approached Parnassus sublime,
Or is it perhaps just a molehill they climb?
Have they with others who fight for the new
Humanity furthered, or just stopped what grew?
Have they sowed peace, or stirred up a storm?
Have they caused heaven or a new hell to form?
In one thing they stand on victorious ground,
Theirs is this day, their hour does sound.
The moor can go, a new play will run,
They dominate the scene, their turn has begun.

"Ja, Ja," the old man mused under his breath as he looked out the window at a small boy who was waving an American flag at a passing car.

"What did you say, Papa?" his daughter asked, looking up from her sewing.

"Nothing; nothing at all," the old man answered in a choked voice. "Go get the wine and some glasses. I want to drink a toast."

Auf Wiedersehen
1946

"Are you sure you have everything?" Frieda Kreutz asked her son. Her voice was low, but one could tell that she was trying to keep all emotion out of its tone.

"Everything I'll need, Mama," Karl answered in an equally studied neutral tenor, as he glanced again at the contents of the open trunk.

All the family had struggled to maintain this stoicism ever since Karl had first received orders that he was to go to Germany as a member of the American occupation forces. Christmas Eve, a week ago, had been especially difficult. As usual, Martin Kreutz, his two sisters, and their families had gathered at the old Kreutz home. After the death of the elder Mrs. Kreutz, the house had been closed and was re-opened only on those occasions when it was traditional with the family to assemble there.

The party had been the smallest of the family reunions which Karl could remember having attended. There had been Aunt Amalie and Uncle Fred Bracht and their unmarried daughters, Annalies and Johanne. Annalies taught in the local high school, and Johanne gave private voice lessons. All the others of Karl's generation were absent. Franz Bracht was an army engineer in Japan and had recently been commissioned colonel. Elsbeth Bracht Wilson was with her parents-in-law awaiting the return of her husband from the European Theater. Aunt Anna and Uncle Viktor were there, but their three daughters spent Christmas Eve of odd-numbered years in town with their husbands' families.

Consequently, the dining table had had to be decreased in size by several leaves, and the Christmas spirit shrank with it. Christmas just wasn't Christmas without old people and little children. With clever place cards and party favors, Frieda Kreutz had tried to make up for the festive air which was lacking, but Christmas Eve 1945 was little more than a tragi-comic travesty for the Kreutzes.

Karl's most disconcerting problem was the attempt to veil the tremendous elation he felt, because it would hurt his parents to know he was glad to be leaving home. As for Martin and Frieda, their only son's departure, perhaps for years, was an event which demanded the greatest restraint which they had ever been called upon to exercise. Of course, the war was over, and Karl would be exposed to little hazard. But their apprehensiveness was occasioned by another sort of concern. Try as he might, Karl could not completely hide his happiness at leaving behind him everything familiar, the places and the people among which he had spent most of the nearly twenty-three years of his life.

Karl had always wanted to go to Europe, ever since he had been old enough to read about the beauties of the old countries. The greatest disappointment of his life had been the necessity for postponing the vacation on the Continent which the family had planned as Karl's high school graduation gift. The war had made that impossible, just as it had interrupted his college education.

"Hadn't you better get ready for the dance? It's eight o'clock," Frieda was saying.

"I guess so," Karl responded. He wasn't looking forward to being with all those people, but he had let his mother persuade him to go to the reunion party which the graduates of the local high school held annually at the Faust Hotel. Oh, well. After tonight he would probably never have to see any of those people again.

Secretly Karl believed he would never return to live in America if Europe were half so wonderful as he imagined it to be. He hated the drabness, the unstimulating provinciality which he thought characterized his hometown. Once he had imagined that living in a big city, New York or San Francisco perhaps, would solve his problem, but his being stationed in several American metropolitan areas had shattered even this last illusion about the acceptability of life in his native country. There was a crass commercialism about the culture, a nerve-grinding rush about the pace of these urban civilizations that was as incompatible with his nature as the stolid conventionalism of the little town where he had grown up.

As Karl Kreutz stood before the mirror tying his cravat, he again experienced that strange fascination which he had always felt when looking at his reflection or photographs of himself. He was not vain about his appearance, though he was handsome in a rather cool way. He was principally interested in how he looked, because he felt there should somehow be more in his face and physical attitude to reveal the incongruities of his nature. Instead his whole semblance bespoke harmony and placidity. This deceptive affability was one of his greatest assets in performing his duties as an officer in the army. It helped to counter-balance his youthfulness and his unmilitary behavior.

"I won't be late," Karl called to his mother as he started to go outside. "I hope Papa comes in from the pasture before long so that you won't be alone."

"It's all right," Frieda said. "I'll get used to it sooner or later."

There was something so intensely sad about the woman as she said the words that Karl felt himself compelled to go over to where she sat holding an open book in her lap.

"I'm sorry, Mama," he said, his voice trembling. Her hand in his was small and frail by contrast, but their shapes were very much alike. They had the same slender fingers which arched gently up from the second joint, and the same long, oval nails. Her free hand went to her son's freshly shaven cheek.

"My little boy," she said, and the tears made her eyes sparkle in the light which filtered through the rose-colored silk lampshade at her side. "Run along now and join your friends. The girls will be waiting for you," she urged, trying to sound gay.

"Remember when you taught me to dance?" Karl recalled. "You're still the best waltz partner in the world." And after kissing his mother swiftly he rushed out of the room as if pursued.

The winter night was clear as Karl went out to the garage to get the car. He could never stand here atop the hill without feeling a peculiar exaltation and fear, as if he were in the presence of a power he could not explain. For miles around, in every direction except to the southeast, he could see nothing but his father's land, thousands of acres of pasture and fields. It was discomfiting to be sole heir to all this wealth and not to know what to do with it.

Karl loved the ranch for what it meant to his father and had meant to his grandfather. He loved it for its beauty and its aristocratic aloofness and because it would someday be his own. But he did not want it, because it incorporated all the responsibilities and conservatism he wanted to escape. Land is the source of all power and of all enslavement, he thought to himself. It is permanence, security, and immutability. It is roots, and I am a tumbleweed.

The lights of the town made the valley look like a giant theater marquee in a foreign alphabet. Karl got into the automobile and coasted all the way to the foot of the hill. When he noticed that the car was slowing down, he stepped on the accelerator and maneuvered the powerful machine into town.

The Evangelical Church clock was striking nine as Karl parked the car next to the hotel and got out. The orchestra was already playing in the ballroom, and some people were dancing. Others were gathered in the lobby in conversational groups when Karl walked in. Slowly he removed his officer's cap and overcoat and handed them to one of the negro attendants, lighted a cigarette, and glanced about the room in search of familiar faces. After three years away in the army, he felt even more a stranger in his home town than he had before the war.

Suddenly an arm slipped around his, and a feminine voice said, "Hello, Karl! I was hoping you would come."

It was his cousin, Annalies Bracht, tall and fashionably sleek in a severe chartreuse gown, with her ash-blond hair piled on top of her head in mussel-like swirls. Karl could never look at Annalies these days without remembering her as a chubby little girl with pigtails which he had cut off one day, forcing her to wear her hair in a boyish bob for months. To look at her no one would ever guess she was a small-town sociology teacher.

"Let's go sit somewhere and talk," Karl hastened to suggest, hoping to avoid the necessity of renewing his acquaintance with a lot of former schoolmates about whom he cared less than nothing.

"Okay," Annalies said, "but first I want you to meet Dr. Cunningham. He's new in town, and I invited him to the reunion. There he is," she said as he looked toward the door where a young man stood smoking a cigarette. "Come here, Tom. I want you to meet my cousin."

Introductions were made, and Karl found himself managing to smile and be almost cordial to the stranger.

"How about joining us in a drink, Lieutenant?" Dr. Cunningham asked Karl. "I have some terrific scotch up in my room on the second floor."

"Sure thing," Karl answered a bit hesitantly, wondering who was meant by "us." Annalies had already gone to push the button for the elevator. How things had changed! A few years ago a young lady would not have dared go to a man's hotel room, even if chaperoned by her cousin. Not in this town. And Annalies was, he knew, one of the least likely people in the world to do anything which might be considered scandalous.

The three got out of the elevator and went into the doctor's room at the end of the corridor.

"Nice room you have here, doctor," Karl said as he glanced about.

"Let's drop the formality, shall we? Call me Tom," the doctor invited. "Annalies does." There was an exchange of very warm glances between him and the girl.

Karl could not understand his own embarrassment. Am I getting to be a prude, he asked himself. Surely not! I brushed up against a lot of rather shady business in the army, and here I am acting like the star Sunday-school pupil, because a man and a girl look at each other meaningfully over highballs in his hotel room.

Annalies took a cigarette out of the glass box on the table and calmly lighted it as she leaned her head against the upholstered back of the chair in which she sat.

"What's the matter, Karl?" she asked quizzically. "You act as though you had just swallowed a goldfish or something."

"I guess I just can't help wondering what the school board would think if they could see you," Karl responded seriously.

Tom Cunningham and Annalies laughed heartily and without artificiality.

"The school board is made up of intelligent men, Karl," Annalies said. "They hired me because I was a human being, a perfectly normal young woman. They want the children of the town to be taught by well balanced individuals, not by straight-laced oldmaids who picture life as a rather dull experience in which knowing the types of crustacea is more important than knowing how to get along with people."

"They know you smoke and take a drink occasionally?" Karl asked incredulously.

"Of course," Annalies chuckled. "And they know that a very attractive young doctor takes me to dinner and dancing when he has the time to spare."

"But this town used to be so . . . so conventional!" Karl stammered.

"It still is," Annalies explained, "but the conventions have changed. When people get shuffled around as much as they have in the last few years, things are bound to change, even here."

"Not to change the subject," Tom Cunningham interrupted, "but I have to make a call on one of my Mexican patients. Would you like to come along?"

"I would," Annalies said eagerly. "How about you, Karl?"

"Why . . . why, yes," Karl answered. "Why not?" He didn't especially want to go to the dance downstairs anyway.

There were other people in the elevator as Annalies and her two escorts got in. Karl recognized one of them as Johnny Preis, who used to sit next to him in algebra class.

"Hi, Johnny!" he said warmly. "It's good to see you, boy. Where have you been?"

What did he care where Johnny Preis had been? Why was he being so darned cordial? He knew perfectly well one drink couldn't make that much difference in his behavior.

"Karl, Karl Kreutz! You old son of a gun! How in the world are you?" Johnny was almost shouting as he gave Karl a sound slap on the shoulder.

What had come over everybody? Karl wondered. He had never been on very intimate terms with the other man, and here they were acting like long separated brothers.

"I'm going out for a little while, but I'll be back," Karl told Johnny. "See you then."

"Don't you forget it," Johnny said. "You were always a great one for forgetting."

What in the world was he referring to? Karl wondered. It could have only one meaning. Johnny meant the time that he had invited Karl to go fishing with him. Then at the last minute Karl had decided not to go, because he hated to have to admit he couldn't row a boat. Later he had told Johnny he had forgotten when they were to go. Looking back at his school days, Karl could remember dozens of such instances where he had rejected the opportunity to make friends with boys of his age. It was small wonder that he never had had a gang like most boys, he admitted to himself.

"Here's my car," Tom Cunningham announced.

Karl held the door open for Annalies and sat down next to her.

"It's a beautiful night, isn't it?" Annalies commented.

"Yeah," Tom agreed. "Not so good if you have diphtheria. That's why I'm making this call. The little girl I'm going to see is just recovering from it."

"You see, Karl," Annalies said. "Tom takes care of the bodies, and I take care of the minds. Some of our cases overlap."

"Who takes care of the spirits?" Karl asked cynically. The devotion of his two companions to their professions seemed a little foolish to him, though he envied them their purposefulness.

"Funny thing," Tom said. "The spirit usually takes care of itself, if a man will give it a chance."

The words resounded in Karl's ears like a whisper in an empty cathedral. Give it a chance. Give it a chance. Had he ever given himself a chance? When friendship had been offered, he had rejected it because of timidity. He had always dreaded getting attached to things for fear they would be snatched away. It had been the same way with people. He had preferred being called a sissy to playing with the other boys. He might have grown to like it. He had never dated the same girl more than a few times, because if she was nice enough to take out at all she could make herself mean something to him. He had never let himself get really interested in any line of work, because he had before him the constant example of his father working from early till late and growing old and tired without having enough time to notice.

"Say, I've never noticed that before," Tom Cunningham said, pointing to the building which they were passing. "The courthouse has four entrances."

"I only know of three," Karl said. "Where is the other one?"

"It's at the back," Annalies explained. "The plans for the building were drawn for the town square. One door was to open to each of the four sides. Then it was decided the court-house would be put on the corner instead of on the plaza. But there had been some juggling of bids, and the building contract had already been given to the architect with the four-door plan. So the back door leads into an empty lot, and nobody uses it. Hardly anybody even knows it exists."

"It's strange that I should have lived here all my life without knowing that," Karl mused. There was so much he evidently did not know about his home town.

"You ought to know about that," Annalies said. "Papa told me that our Grandfather Kreutz wrote a perfectly scorching letter to the newspaper when it happened, berating the county officers for their mismanagement. Papa says that Opa Kreutz was always one of the most civic-minded people he had ever known."

Karl cringed inwardly. He felt that Annalies was deliberately making him uncomfortable, trying to make him feel he was not living up to the family tradition of public-spirited citizenship.

"Tell me, Karl," Tom asked, "are half the things Annalies says about the family true? If I didn't know her so well, I'd think she was bragging."

"I don't know what she has been saying," Karl answered laughingly, "but our ancestors *were* quite illustrious."

"It isn't that so much that I'm proud of," Annalies insisted. "It's the way they managed to be content and useful wherever they were. They must have had a hard time adjusting themselves to conditions on the frontier after being accustomed to European court life. They just created their own cultural and social worlds around them from almost nothing."

"You sound like a sociology textbook," Karl teased. But every word Annalies said dug itself into his consciousness like a fish hook.

"Well, here we are," Tom announced. "You all wait for me. I'll be back out in a few minutes."

Karl and Annalies sat quietly for a moment. Then Annalies spoke.

"You'll be leaving tomorrow morning."

"Yes," Karl said, trying to re-capture the joy he had felt earlier in the evening whenever he had thought of the trip he was about to take.

"I envy you, but I don't guess it will be a pleasure jaunt," she declared. "I've always thought that perhaps in Germany I would find something that seems to be lacking here. But I'm afraid that all those wonderful things have changed forever. Culture doesn't thrive on empty stomachs and in rubbish heaps."

There was nothing for Karl to say. The truth of what she had said was as indisputable as it was painful.

"Awhile ago, when you were telling about the courthouse and how it happened to have four doors, I couldn't help thinking it was rather like me. I've always felt I wasn't made for the place I filled," Karl said.

"All of us who grow up between two cultures feel a little out of key with things at times," Annalies said. "It takes time. We aren't quite integrated yet."

"Do you feel that way too?" Karl said. "I thought I was the only one who had a closed door. It's been there all the time, but almost no one knows about it. It just leads to emptiness and serves no purpose except to remind me that I don't fit where I am."

"That door isn't always closed, Karl," Annalies corrected.

"Sometimes, when the air gets stuffy, they open it to let the breeze through. If the city would just use the empty lot, make a garden of it, think how lovely it would be, hidden away from the noise of the streets but open to anyone who wanted to come there to relax."

Evidently Annalies had chosen to ignore his simile. Or had she? Karl thought. Open the door, Karl, she seemed to have said. Open the door and cultivate the recesses of your mind. Open the door and let in the breeze. Annalies would not put it that way, because she was a practical person, not inclined to speak poetically. But there was poetry in this practical idea.

"Well, the child's temperature is coming back to normal," Tom said as he got into the car. Shall we go back to the dance?"

"Yes, let's," Karl said, his attention still a bit befogged by his conversation with his cousin.

"It's a beautiful night," Annalies said with a sigh.

"You've said that before," Tom reminded her laughingly.

"I know. But it's still a beautiful night," Annalies repeated with a smile.

"It certainly is," Karl agreed with genuine gaiety in his voice.

The trip back took only a few minutes, during which the three young people silently enjoyed one another's company. When they reached the scene of the party, Karl remembered his promise to Johnny Preis, so he excused himself, and the young couple danced away. After a moment of searching he found Johnny and a girl sitting together in the lobby having cigarettes and talking.

"I might have known you'd be with a girl," Karl called, trying to strike the same informal, flippant key which had so mysteriously characterized their meeting earlier in the evening.

"Loraine, this is Karl Kreutz," Johnny said to the young woman at his side. "Karl, my sister, Loraine Fields."

Karl's embarrassment at having committed a faux pas was exceeded only by his immediate interest in Johnny's sister. Since their names weren't the same, he thought, she must be married. But she wasn't wearing a wedding ring. There was a little white space on the correct finger where a ring must have been until recently. While he made these observations, Karl had managed to acknowledge the introduction with a simple "How do you do."

"I remember you," Loraine was saying, "though obviously you don't know me."

"I'm afraid . . . " Karl was growing more self-conscious every moment.

"Don't apologize," Loraine graciously interrupted him. "I was two grades behind you and Johnny, but I remember once, at the closing exercises of the German summer school that the Sons of Hermann used to sponsor, you recited Schiller's 'Der Taucher.' You were wonderful!" she concluded with a little hyperbolic facial expression which would have made most people seem theatrical. She merely seemed very charming and as sincere as a child.

"You remember that?" Karl said in amazement. "Why, that must have been ten years ago at least!"

"I remember it because I was to play a piece on the piano right after you recited. And as you walked off and I was about to go on, you said, 'Don't be scared. It's not as bad as you think.' And you were shaking like a leaf!"

The three young people laughed, and as if their laughter had beckoned, several other people who had been sitting nearby came over to join the little group who sat on the sofa by the window.

Karl was surprised to see how many of the people he recognized and could call by name after not having seen them in several years. More puzzling to him was the easy, informal manner in which he found himself conversing with his old schoolmates. It was as if they had forgotten how they had called him a sissy in the grades and a playboy in high school and college. Now he was just one of them, a young officer on leave in his hometown. Only enough of their common pasts was remembered to make conversation a simple matter. There was a poise and worldliness about the men and the girls which made it hard for Karl to realize that they were people he had known all his life. With equal facility they talked of new books, politics, music, and the places they had been. It could have been any group of intelligent young people anywhere, except that occasionally they would drop back into the German idiom for a sentence or two. Some had been to college, some had not. A few were from the old prominent families, but most of them were the children of the town's insurance agents and storekeepers and laborers. Several were boys and girls from mill town or the Mexican village. Except for these last it was hard to tell which were which. Suddenly Annalies' words came to Karl.

"They created their cultural and social world around them from almost nothing." And then the words of Tom Cunningham: "The spirit usually takes care of itself, if a man will give it a chance." Open the door, Karl. Open the door!

"Shall we dance, Loraine?" he asked the young woman who sat beside him.

"Why, yes, thanks," she responded with a smile that said she had been wishing he would ask her. But as they danced, he felt her body grow tense in his arms.

"Would you prefer we sit this one out?" he asked considerately.

"Yes. Yes, I guess so," she answered, her voice quivering

uncertainly. He steered her out to the patio, away from the crowd.

"Would I be prying if I asked what's the matter?" he asked when she seemed to have relaxed a bit.

"No. No, of course not," she said. "It's just that this is the first time I have gone out among people here since my divorce."

"I'm sorry," he said quietly. He knew her very slightly, but it hurt him to see her unhappy.

"It's all right," she responded as if consoling him. "It just didn't work out, that's all. Bob and I never understood each other. He loved the big cities and he didn't want a home and family. For him there was absolutely no glamour in familiar things."

It seemed to Karl that everything people said tonight applied to him. It was as if everyone had conspired to take this last opportunity to tell him his own faults disguised as those of others.

"It's not that I don't have any desire to travel, or that I want to settle back into a monotonous existence. Life can't be entirely dull unless one is a very dull person. But I want to feel I belong somewhere," she concluded.

There it was again. The old story of having one's niche, of being a part of something.

In the background the lights were dimming, and the orchestra struck up "Auld Lang Syne." The dancers had stopped moving about and were singing. Karl and Loraine were alone in the shadows of the potted palms. It was the perfect setting for a kiss. The thought hadn't occurred to him before, and now that it had, he rejected it. It seemed such an adolescent way in which to start their relationship. When he got back, she would have come to know him better through letters.

When he came back! He took her hand and held it firmly in his as they stood in the darkness listening to the sentimental old song. The music stopped and the lights were turned up again.

"Well," he said with a regretful sigh, "everyone is leaving, and I'll have to take you back to Johnny. It's been a wonderful evening. And remember, don't be scared. It's not as bad as you think."

Together they laughed at their private joke as they went back indoors to find Loraine's brother.

"Good-bye, Karl," Johnny said as he helped his sister into her coat. "Good luck, too. Let us hear from you." The two men shook hands with a warmth which was new to Karl.

"You'll hear from me, never fear," Karl responded. "This is just auf Wiedersehen."

Yes, it was indeed a beautiful night, and the sleeping town was beautiful too as he left it behind him and ascended the hill. Karl looked all around him at the land which would someday be his own. There was none of the old fear as he considered the prospect of carrying on the work which his Grandfather Kreutz had begun. He would be leaving tomorrow, to be gone for a while. But tonight he felt completely at peace among the oaks whose deep-rooted trunks cast stately shadows around him. The only sound was that of the breeze in their branches singing a melody to the accompaniment of the throbbing beat of his heart.

Karl walked into the familiar house and without hesitation found his way to his mother's bedside. As usual she was awake when he came in.

"You can go to sleep now, Mama," he whispered as he kissed her good-night. "I've finally come home."

About the Author

Minetta Altgelt Goyne was born in 1924 into a family remarkably similar to the Kreutz clan. After taking a degree in German from the University of Texas, Ms. Goyne (then Miss Minetta Altgelt) began graduate study in both English and German. The stories in this collection were presented to the university's graduate faculty as a master's thesis in creative writing in 1946 under the title "Though the Old Call." In 1947, Miss Altgelt married A. V. Goyne, Jr., and in 1949 the Goynes became the parents of a son. Twenty-one years after receiving her M.A. from the University of Texas, Minetta Goyne returned to complete a doctorate in German literature. TCU Press published her *Lone Star and Double Eagle: Civil War Letters of a German-Texas Family* in 1982, and Texas A&M Press her *A Life Among the Texas Flora: Ferdinand Lindheimer's Letters to George Engelmann* in 1991. Ms. Goyne taught variously at the University of Texas, Texas Christian University, Louisiana State University, Texas Wesleyan University, and the University of Texas at Arlington. Minetta Altgelt Goyne died on October 21, 1992.